Fancy a Coffee?

DIPANJANA NATH

INDIA • SINGAPORE • MALAYSIA

ISBN 979-8-89233-843-1

Contents

First Story: Soulmates

Chapter 1

Clotted clouds and heavy downpour flushed even the broadways, causing flash floods and a chilly wind. It seemed like a severe winter was hovering over us, and frostbites were about to slay their cruel chafes on our skin. Raindrops rolled down the glossy sidings of our cafeteria's sash windows, but my gaze was lost staring out at the mangrove trees. I wondered how those trees managed to stand so high, facing the adverse weather. Romance was taking a backseat, and philosophy took over my mind. A silhouette of my friend cum colleague, Pallavi, flashed at the corner of my focus. Her turtlenecked purple top, paired with a white skirt, looked perfect for a cozy winter afternoon. She was lean, but with a curvy hip area, and hence the skirt took on a beautiful mermaid shape. My dowdy look gave her instant irritation, and I could see the frustration on Pallavi's face. "Hi babe!" Her phone clattered on the wooden table, and she yanked open the lunchbox, oozing out a strong aroma of onions and mushrooms.

"Just coffee? Don't tell me you are dieting. There's hardly anything left in there!" She asked me, rolling her broad eyes. Her expressions scanned me from head to toe.

I smiled, lopsided, somehow reluctant to reply.

A strong pinch on my forearm brought me back to reality.

"Ouch! Stop it!" I batted away her lavender-painted nails.

"Come on, Shama! Should I go to a different table, darling?" She said, I could see that she was seated with a scornful expression and had already downed a spoonful of mushrooms.

I forced a smile on my lips. She pulled a face. My gaze traced back to the trees.

My name is Shama, Shama Rangarajan, and Pallavi has been my best friend since my college days; now, we are colleagues. We both moved to the USA for higher studies and ended up working at the same software firm in the northwestern suburb of Illinois. Pallavi was a jovial and high-spirited woman in her thirties, and so was I. Until a week ago, even I dolled up myself with fine attire and styled my hair, but that day I was feeling low, kind of out of my mind. My appetite was lost, and I was surviving only on coffee. Two sleepless nights and a few shots of rum were still reminding me strongly of my ex-beloved's wedding.

"Come on, girl! Snap out of it! Let me grab a sandwich for you." Pallavi shoved the spoon back into her mushroom rice and got to her feet, cocking her head toward the cash counter to check if the counter was open or if it had already shut since it was nearing closing time.

"I'm not hungry, Pallavi! And my situation is not as bad as you are thinking! So chill!" I pulled her hand, making her flump right back into her seat.

"My nails!" she screamed, double-checking her freshly fixed faux nails. I smiled broadly, but she probably found out the fakeness of my smile.

"Listen, Shama, I understand that you had to go through a bad breakup, and the guy who you thought was an angel came out to be a jerk! But that's life! Come on, girl! You need to move on!" She lectured, even though I was not at all in the mood to listen or follow anything that was coming my way.

"I know! I'm not telling that I would be stuck in him forever, but come on, it definitely needs some time to forget a person, right?" I frowned my brows, agitated this time.

"Hmm… Yup! But what's the logic of starving until you forget him? Let's do one thing!" she jiggled.

"What?" I pulled my face, thinking she was definitely coming up with some weird ideas of hooking me up with some new guy. I probably knew her better than her parents by now.

"Not again, Pallavi!" I warned.

"No… no! I was going to talk about matching the sun signs and moon signs to find a Prince for you." Her joke irritated me further.

"Hey, aren't you guys coming for the meeting?" our colleague Thomas hastily knocked the back of my chair while walking along the cafeteria aisle. He was on his way toward the conference hall across the cafeteria for our weekly update meeting.

"Shoot!" a chorus voice from Pallavi and me came aloud, and we strode fast, rushing our way to our cubicles to grab laptops and notes.

Two weeks later:

It was a cold, sunny morning. I got off the usual train that took me from the suburb to downtown Chicago, and then I planned for a brief walk to enjoy the frosty weather. The morning chill pierced my cheeks like a thousand needles, and I took a halt at the bus stop located at the junction of Madison and South Canal Street. My idea of a small walk along the Chicago River was doomed, and the thought that a half jacket would be sufficient to block the cold weather from penetrating my skin was wrong.

It was five minutes to nine, and I saw two men walking from the other side of the road. They crossed the street and walked toward me. One of them wore a nice blue jacket, but the other person wore just a formal shirt tucked into a pair of formal pants. The silky thread of his shirt glistened under the sun rays as they stopped right in front of me, at the same bus stop.

Same office?

My mind voice echoed, and I found the shirt guy's eyes drifting back and forth to see me. His sunglasses that covered his eyes had a deep shade of navy blue, but they were semi-transparent. I could see him staring at me, on and off. He rubbed his palm and covered his ears with his palm as a rush of breeze blew our way.

"Would you like to use my earmuffs?" I cracked a conversation, offering him my earmuffs.

"Thank you! But that's alright; I can manage!" He grinned, his perfect set of teeth flashing a smile. But his friend suddenly looked utterly conscious, as if someone throttled his neck in his nightmare.

"It's alright! You can take it. I am not using it anyway!" I shuddered. Moreover, I think you both are headed to the same office! So you can return it once we reach!" I further added, reaching out the earmuffs to him.

"Thank you so much! That's really kind of you!" he took the earmuffs from my clutch and covered his ears quickly with it.

"My name is Samuel Jacobs. By the way, how did you know that we're going to the same office?" he looked into my eyes, looking for a reply. His palms rubbed against each other again.

"I read the logo printed on your backpack! I'm Shama, by the way." I replied with a smile. The other guy finally nodded with a grin.

"I'm Karthik!" he said.

Our bus arrived, and we all boarded the bus quickly, saving ourselves from staying out in the brittle weather.

Samuel's gaze was obvious on me, which kind of made me feel a bit odd too. Once we reached our office, we all got down through the rear door of the bus. He thanked me, returning my earmuffs. I acknowledged. His smile was adorable, and his gesture was manly. My eyes trailed his footsteps on the way to the elevator. He took the first elevator from the hallway, and Karthik and I waited for the second elevator that went to a different entrance, on the same floor. I smiled internally, internalizing the truth that that morning I had hardly thought about my break-up. I wanted to share my accidental yet delightful encounter with Samuel with Pallavi, but unfortunately, I knew that she had taken the day off.

Half the day was over, and I felt terrible thinking about being solo again. On the way to the restroom, I saw Samuel again. He was involved in talking to someone over the phone while striding across the hall. I felt a little strange about bumping into him for the second time on the same day, but when I was about to take the stairs to the café, a holler from behind stopped my move.

"Hey, Shama! Wait!" It was Samuel.

Wow! He remembers my name!

My inner voice tweaked, and I turned around.

"Hey, Samuel! What a surprise!" I drummed up a talk as if I had not seen him standing there.

"First of all, call me 'Sam'. All my friends do, and the second thing is you did see me there, didn't you?" He sounded flirtatious, winking an eye, which gave an involuntary grin on my face.

"Umm… yes! I just didn't want to disturb you." We walked together chugging up the stairs and reached the café and started checking out the meals for that day.

He walked along the counters but didn't pick any item. I did, a quarter portion of rotisserie chicken, white meat, and a side of mixed veggies, tossed in olive oil and white sesame seeds.

"So, aren't you hungry? Why don't you pick something?" I asked him, handing over the card to the lady at the counter.

"No, I'm fine, on a diet!" He winked again as we walked to a table. The first time I blushed to myself, feeling special after a long time.

"Thank you so much for accompanying me! Most of my colleagues are working from home today." I took a bite of the delicious chicken and sipped water from a white paper cup.

"It's completely my pleasure. How long have you been working here?" He darted his next question.

Our casual conversation went on for forty-five minutes. Small talks, jokes, laughter, and occasional intense glances completed the lunch. On our way back, in the empty corridor, he came closer than usual, bringing his nose close to my neck. I turned around a little blush on my lips.

That was fast!

I thought. But I was getting attracted to his daunting handsome look.

"I love your smell!" His fingers brushed my neck, pretending to move a stray hair, but I could very well understand what it indicated. Whatever it was, I wanted it to linger. I could feel a spark between us.

We bade bye to each other as I walked past the strong door of my engineering lab. Through the glass wall, I could still see him, and I saw him looking at me as well.

Pallavi was off for three subsequent days, and that gave me plenty of time to mingle with Sam.

After two more days of lunch together and sharing seats on the same office roamer up and down, I started to feel more attracted toward him. He loved my eyes, my lips, and my baby pink lip stain. He told me that it looked very natural and cute on me. He even brushed his fingers on my lips once in the elevator on the way to the top floor when only we two were left in the elevator and the rest exited. A series of butterflies fluttered in my stomach, and the back of my throat moaned. A pleasure ran down my spine, clutching the inner core of my muscles. He kissed me, but I pushed him softly, nodding in denial. He pulled me closer again, and we kissed passionately. My philosophy of adverse weather and the practicality of life flew out of the window, and once again, romance took a front seat. I was waiting to talk to Pallavi about Samuel, but I could talk to her only after the long weekend. She was off to Hawaii with her family, and hence I didn't want to barge into her private time.

That weekend, at Sam's friend's restaurant:

Sam's friend, Vineeth, ushered us to the cozy seating area as Sam and I maneuvered through the fancy bar stools and the tables. We settled ourselves in the soft plush of a loveseat. Vineeth was a pure gentleman, nice and tall with a very subtle yet happy gesture. He spent a good couple of minutes with us before getting busy with the rest of the guests. It was a long weekend and it seemed like they were hosting a few small private parties as well.

I loved the way the whole thing was going. The ambience was soothing the way I preferred it. Being with Sam felt like a perfect dream. I tried to put my best effort into looking gorgeous in his eyes. A sheath lavender dress with matching ensembles and a pair of pointed heels adorned me. My off-shoulder dress exposed my neck and shoulder, making my skin accessible for a flirty fondle.

Sam fawned over me every now and then and wrapped his arm around my waist. I could feel his warm breath on my shoulder. We shared a bottle of Merlot, cheese cubes, fish, and chips, completing the dish with a mixed veggie salad.

"What happened? Why are you staring?" I smiled, catching his intense gaze.

He nodded. Another wink. I insisted he share the secret behind the shine of his eyes.

"I wanna make love to you!" He whispered and my heart thumped.

"What?" I mouthed, gaping in shock. I saw that coming but not so soon.

"You asked me, so I had to tell you. You're taking my breath away, and there's no point in lying!" He took another sip from his drink. His eyes looked around and stopped on me again. My mind tweaked.

"And what if I wasn't good-looking?" I said, a bit concerned to know a serious reply. He avoided replying; instead, he skimmed through my shoulder, his fingers traveling to my back tracing the lace of my dress. I felt wine in my nerves.

"Hey, I'll be back." I got to my feet and walked across the huge hall to the restroom area. My head spun from the loud music.

When I came out of the restroom, a tall mirror across the restroom nook attracted me, and I walked close to that. I stood right in front of the mirror. The antique design around the spotless mirror matched with the rest of the wall hangings. I looked around and adjusted my attire, making everything look in place, and then played with my hair, styling them in different ways. Suddenly, the mirror opened, and a hand pulled me in. It pulled me into a room.

What the hell?

Someone closed my mouth with a strong grip as we entered into a room.

Chapter 2

The room was dimly lit. I was about to scream at the top of my lungs but then found Samuel standing right in front of me. "What's happening?" I shivered in panic.

"Nothing… calm down," he said, and I took a breath. An aroma of fresh linen rushed through my nose. He was smelling heavenly in a neatly ironed tucked-up shirt and a pair of jeans. His kempt hair was gelled up to give perfect spikes, and his hand wrapped around my waist.

"Hey… what are you trying to do? Why did you bring me here?" My inner core was trying to process the whole thing. I was not ready for sex yet.

Why is it happening so fast!

"You look beautiful!" He touched my cheek. His face was hardly an inch away from mine, and I could feel the minty fresh smell of his breath.

"You are like a tsunami!" I said, "Why don't we give it some more time?" My fingers rubbed his cheeks. I was high on wine.

"It's too early, let's slow it down, please!" I added further, trying to gently pull myself away. "And what place is this? I was in the restroom…how did you get here?" I wondered, my eyes tried to find the answers in his eyes.

"It's their walk-in closet, not a mirror... and why early? I like you and you like me. I can see the same urge in your eyes, lady!" He said, holding my shoulders in his warm grip. I glanced around to see the closet. It looked more like a usual room to me than a walk-in closet.

"Still!" I murmured. The room was neat with mostly linens, some decorative items and dry flowers which smelled deliciously good. A few beautiful candles and bamboo lampshades were stacked up in the corner of the room, and a few pieces of pottery gave the room an earthy finish. Samuel's finger rubbed through my lips, indulging me in togetherness. Even though I was not really up for that intimacy that evening, I gave in after his seductive touch on my body. He kissed me, and I kissed him back with passion. He stroked his fingers on me, and I moaned deeply; our breaths shot faster than ever. He scooped me into his arm gently and made his way to the small sofa bed. Our clothes fell helplessly on the floor, and we made love. We went wilder and wilder as his moist touch maneuvered through every nerve of my body, every inch of my skin. After a prolonged romance and lovemaking, I rested on his arm, and he cocked his head toward me with a witty smile. We kissed again.

When Samuel asked me to pass his jeans, I felt something circular and metallic in his pocket. I took it out, and it shone under the gleam of the dim light. And then it blew my senses.

It was a ring.

I was literally numb.

"Are you married, Sam?" I asked, curious, my eyes darted at him demanding an explanation.

"Ahh... umm!" He mouthed something which hardly reached my ear.

"Of course, you are married! Wow! I was such a fool!" I fumed in agony.

Fuck!

My inner core screamed. But I kept silent, waiting for an answer.

"Hey Shama, I like you! And how does it matter whether I'm married or not? I like you and you like me, and isn't that enough for us to spend time together?" He reached my slumped shoulder and gave them a rub, but I shrugged his hands off.

"How can you take things so granted? How can you hide the fact from me? If you are looking for a 'no strings attached' kind of relationship, you should've bloody well made that clear before you jumped into bed with me." Tears rolled down, and I stomped out of the room with my shoes in my hand. Two of the waiters stared at me as I tried to flaunt a smile at them and rushed out of the restaurant on bare feet.

Next day:

"Are you mad at me because I didn't tell you about my long weekend plan?" Pallavi peeped over my shoulder looking into my computer screen.

"Are you going to be shadowing me for the whole day?" I said, my eyes on the screen.

She turned the revolving chair of mine, and I faced her.

"Why do you look so pale? What's the matter?" She took my hands in a friendly squeeze. A drop of tear rolled down, wetting my black skirt.

"Let's go for a coffee break!" She pulled me along, and I walked like a heartbroken teenager following her to the cafeteria.

Over two rounds of coffee, I shared my story with Pallavi, and she fumed in agony listening to the whole thing.

"Wow! You know what? I know that guy, and I also know that he was married! I should have been here with you!" Pallavi narrowed her eyes. "But whatever it is, he shouldn't have hidden the fact from you!" She exhaled a snort of disgust. "Anyways, he doesn't deserve any space in your memory stack!" Pallavi slurped the last bit of her drink with an annoying sound.

"Oh no! Sam is calling!" I murmured, showing her the phone screen. My eyes were still moist.

"Ask him to get lost and hire a professional for his lust habits. We are not up for casual sex!" The word sex kept ringing in my ears.

A month later:

A hardware test was being conducted in our secluded Laboratory. After checking the temperature tolerance of our yet-to-be-released phone, I finally rested myself on one of the revolving stools, shuffling through some pictures on my Facebook account. The phone signal had been really weak in the lab, and hence I shifted toward one of the glass windows. I still had to wait for another twenty minutes for the test to be completed. So I checked the clock again, tired.

A messenger icon flashed on the notification panel of my phone, catching my attention. I short-pressed to open the message when our manager rushed in for a quick stand-up. I shoved my phone back into the pocket of my jeans. My phone kept vibrating, and I kept wondering, guessing who could be the sender. My heart was vexed and frustrated after Samuel's incident, and I swore to God that I'd never fall in love again.

Come on, Samuel if it's you, then this time I'm gonna bloody call your dear wife!

My inner voice echoed. Pallavi eyed me, bringing my attention back to the meeting, and I nodded almost without listening to what our manager exactly said. After he was gone, Pallavi, Thomas, and I had a quick chat lingering on the project topic. A beep sound from the machine reminded me that the test was done. Another vibration from my phone, and I took it out to check.

"Hey, do you remember me?" A message flashed.

Come on! Not again!

The frown on my face caught Pallavi's eyes.

"All ok?" She asked. "Is that Sam?" She poked my hand with her long nail.

"No." But the message made me active suddenly.

I sprang up, got to my feet and walked a little away from Pallavi to check the rest of the message.

The message went like the following:

"Do you remember someone called Ashwin Roy? We used to be Bus mates! We met each other at a bus stop for the first time and then one day, all of a sudden, you disappeared! Do you remember me? If not, please ignore my messages. Thank you!"

I froze for a moment, amazed, thinking.

Ashwin Roy! Come on! Seriously?

My voice echoed within my heart.

More than bus-mates! We used to be best friends during our college days! How did I forget him?

I jumped for joy. Through the glass sidings, the corridor was visible where Samuel just passed by. He smiled at me, and his hand gestures asked me to phone him. I avoided his glance and went back to my computer.

"Should I just call his wife?" Pallavi's voice drifted through, and Thomas stared at her weirdly. "My wife?"

We all broke into a big laughter.

"Hey Ashwin, of course, I remember you! Hope everything is going great at your end! Thank you so much for connecting!" I typed a formal message and sent it across. A smiley came in return. My mind dove into the past thinking about Ashwin Roy. All the old memories which took the rearmost stack in my brain, collecting the layers of new memories, withstanding the blows of time, came alive once again, flashing one by one in front of my eyes.

I smiled, remembering Ashwin's Maggie hair and his cute eyes behind a pair of thick-framed glasses. The incident of our first meeting at the bus stop next to our house flashed in front of my eyes, re-running the incidents when we fell from a bike, when we watched films together, and when we hugged each other. My mind parked at one spot of my memory where all the long-gone incidents came alive one more time.

That evening we fell into a pothole on the way back from our coaching class.

Our bike rides, our evening walks to the beach, watching horror movies together, our chats for long hours standing at the old staircase of our house—everything appeared one by one in front of my eyes over and over again.

After my elder sister's wedding, I shifted to her in-laws' house and totally lost touch with Ashwin.

Why didn't I try to meet him again? I left the city and never even bothered to inform him! He must have wondered, thought how insensitive I was!

My mind questioned me, and I had no answer.

"How about a call tonight? I am very sorry for whatever happened, but I would love to talk to you! So 9 PM tonight?" I typed in the message while packing my stuff while Pallavi waited for me holding the door. We shared the same apartment.

A smiley came in response, and then we were off on the road. Pallavi was driving that day, and I was planning to share our story with her. The story of Ashwin Roy and Shama!

Chapter 3

A decade and a half ago:

It was a rainy day. I yanked out the umbrella from the doornail and scurried out of our apartment building in Shastri Nagar. I was unusually late for college that day. I lived in Shastri Nagar with my elder sister, who was pursuing her nursing certification at the same college where I was doing my engineering. The day was cloudy, and one session of heavy downpours had already made the streets dirty and mud-splattered. I wore my yellow salwar with a matching yellow dupatta, which happened to be one of my favorites during my college days. My hair was still a little damp, and fresh kohl darkened my eye rims with a bold border. My sister sent me off with a goodbye kiss, and I chugged down the stairs, walking briskly toward the bus stop behind our house, right at the turning of the main road.

It started to drizzle again when I kept waiting for the bus. A boy, around my age, walked fast, crossing the almost empty road. Probably, he was trying to save his curly hair from getting wet by holding a newspaper on his head. His thick-framed glasses, Maggie-like hair, and naturally red lips looked very cute on him. He was wearing a light beige-colored shirt and black pants, and a huge backpack hung from his shoulders. I looked at him, flaunting a formal smile, and he smiled back. The roads were deserted, and most people made a smart choice of ditching the heavy rain. I cocked my head to my right over and again to check if there was any bus approaching our stop.

"May I know the time, please?" A subtle voice reached my ear, and I turned to him. He wasn't wearing a watch. And, of course, no cell phone either. The cell phone concept wasn't popular in those days. It was mostly restricted only among elders or rich kids, not in middle-class families.

"It's 8.45 AM." I looked at my white and red Titan watch and then looked at him. He smiled. "Ok. Thanks!"

"Are you waiting for your college bus?" I asked him, prolonging the conversation.

A big honk caught our attention, and our heads turned simultaneously to a bus. Unfortunately, it was one of the Volvo luxury buses and not the usual government transport commutes.

"Crescent College… you?" He said. His curly hair touched the borderline of his shoulders.

"SRM. 3rd year, Engineering," I said, smiling. My eyes were back on the road.

We went quiet again. A few more people joined us at the bus stop, and he moved a little closer to me.

"Which year?" I asked him casually.

"2nd." His short reply came, and I nodded, acknowledging.

Finally, my bus came, and I got in. In a hurry, I forgot to say bye to him, but after finding a seat, I waved at him. I saw his broad grin. He waved back, and we smiled at each other.

There was something very strange in his eyes, very different, very attractive. I thought about it until I reached college, but after that, between the classes, books, and lessons adding on, it became just another usual thought. That day I forgot to ask his name.

After a couple of days, we met again in the same place at the same time. That day, my sister was with me, and she spoke to him more than I did.

"So, what's your name?" she asked curiously.

"Ashwin Roy," he said politely. "And yours?"

"I am Manisha Rangarajan, and she is my sister, Shama." She pointed at me. Ashwin responded, "nice names!"

However, his bus came before ours, and he boarded the bus. Similarly, he took a window seat and waved at us while leaving.

"Cute kid!" my sister said.

"He's almost my age," I said.

"No, he must be younger than you!" she replied.

"Hmm!" I acknowledged, nodding.

Just one year!

My mind's voice echoed.

We started seeing him frequently at the same bus stop. While my sister remained busy talking to her friends, Ashwin and I used to chat a lot about studies, sports, crushes— all kinds of casual, friendly topics.

My sister invited him home later, another day, to watch a horror film with us. By then, we knew that his mother was working as an accountant at a local bank, and his father was a marketing agent. He came home in a royal blue loose shirt and faded blue jeans. The shirt looked too loose for him, but it suited his complexion.

We sat on the divan bed in our living room facing the computer screen with a few bottles of Pepsi and snacks. From right to left: first Ashwin, then I, then my sister, and then our maid—the sitting order was like that. I clutched his arm very tight once or twice during the scary scenes. He joked that I almost ripped off his skin. We spoke standing at the staircase for quite a long time, and then he left.

Ashwin had a bicycle, but he loaned a motorcycle from one of his cousins. I playfully asked him to teach me motorbike, but he took it pretty seriously, and one fine day, he parked his motorbike beneath our house and came and knocked on our door. I literally jumped up in joy and became excited to learn a bike. My sister looked at me in a strange way. Her eyes toggled between me and Ashwin, and finally, she gave us the permission.

"You can ride, but please stay close to home… I should be able to see you both from the balcony!" Sister said, going into a mom mode.

The Beach road close to our house was just a single-stretch broad road. He used to pick me up every other day, and we used to go to the beach. I rode the bike from one end of the road to another end a couple of times, and finally, after the sunset, we used to go for casual walks along the shore. We used to buy steamed peanuts and take long walks to the small fish stalls. I admired the shops that sold shells or shell-made stuff.

After a few of the bike ride episodes, one day, my sister asked me if there was anything going on between Ashwin and me. That question surprised me since I never thought about him that way. "He is a dude friend!" I winked at her. Our maid, Rupa, giving a scalp massage to my sister, tried to figure out what it meant. My sister smiled, hearing the "dude friend" phrase.

During the fourth year of college, on the way to our computer class one day, when we bumped into a pothole after miscalculating the depth of it, we fell hard on the road, hitting our knees on the ground. Skin ripped off, and blood oozed out with a terrible pain. Ashwin fell to the ground, and his head hit against the uneven sidewalk, which scared the hell out of me.

"Are you alright?" My fingers started shaking in fear when I saw his head bleeding.

"I think so!" his eyes appeared unusually droopy. I was scared, thinking what if he passed out. I gave him my dupatta, and he pressed it against his head. It was at the peak of the evening, and luckily, a small clinic was just at the corner on the same road. Few people came running to help. Our condition was not so bad, and we could manage the short walk to the hospital. A known person took the motorcycle and assured us, saying that he would park it in front of his shop. Ashwin nodded. The rest of the crowd got cleared off once they saw us walking to the hospital.

I limped on my right leg, feeling the twist and pain in my knee and ankle. Ashwin felt dizzy from the fall. The small boy from the shop handed us the vehicle keys and also held Ashwin's hand to the hospital.

"I'm ok!" Ashwin said, smiling. I felt relief from his smirk.

After waiting for a couple of minutes in the clinic corridor, the doctor called us in. A short, structured square-faced nurse ushered us in. She cleaned his forehead before the doctor took over. He stitched his forehead with no anesthesia. My heart thumped in fear, but I was surprised to see his courage. Not a single drop of tear in his eyes. I held his hand the whole time of the stitching session. Then the nurse came back, and she asked him to lie down. She asked him to lower his pants so that she could put an injection in his rear.

I turned around, suppressing a snigger.

"Shut up! Don't laugh!" He screamed.

"Sorry!" I said, pursing my lips. But that's when the young nurse laughed, getting him more embarrassed. He was upset for the rest of the evening due to the 'laugh' matter.

His birthday came just before the last semester of my final year. He invited me home for his birthday party. I was a little skeptical about going there since the rest of the guests were from his college, and moreover, they were at least a year younger than me. I tried to avoid it, telling many reasons, but finally, Ashwin felt upset, and hence I felt bad and gave in to his stubbornness. I wore my maroon and white salwar with earrings that had white beads and bangles that were white in color and walked toward his house that evening. His mother opened the door for me and pulled me into a warm hug, welcoming me into their house. She had a very homely appearance and a serene smile. Ashwin had her pair of eyes. She ushered me in and asked me to feel at home.

The living room was packed with his friends, boys, and girls both. Ashwin's face glistened with joy when he saw me and rushed toward me. He pulled my hand and dragged me along to give my intro to his friends. His father spared me an intriguing look.

"Hi guys, this is Shama, my neighbor!" Ashwin announced.

"Hi…" a chorus holler echoed in the room.

His mom walked in with a huge cake and colorful candles lit and placed around the cake. He cut the cake, and we all clapped for him.

I conversed with a few of his friends, mostly girls and also Ashwin, and finally plated my portion of cake and took a stroll to find a secluded place. He got busy talking with friends, and my mind demanded a less noisy place. I settled on their balcony, away from the crowd, in silence, relaxed. Too much noise was never my thing and was mostly overwhelming.

"Hey, what are you doing here? I've been looking for you!" A voice drifted in the air as I looked at the door that led to the balcony. Ashwin stood there.

"Just wanted to enjoy the breeze! Why did you come here leaving the party? Go and enjoy!" I pushed him back toward the door again.

"No! Why are you pushing me? I'm taking a break!" He leaned on the balcony rails, standing next to me.

"It's your day! Btw happy birthday again!" I reached out to shake his hand again. I don't know why, but he lingered in his grip as if he didn't want to let go of my hand, which looked a little strange to me. I smiled. "What?" I asked.

"Nothing!" he replied, his shoulders shrugged. A gentle breeze blew softly as we polished our plates. I tossed the plates into the dustbin kept in the corner between two doors.

"You have a beautiful house!" I said, falling short of topics.

"Thanks!" he smiled.

"I should be leaving now! Didi must be waiting!" I said, and he nodded. He looked quiet, as if something was occupying his mind as if he wanted to say something.

"What?" I asked again, about to leave the balcony.

He abruptly pulled my hands and pulled me closer. His eyes stared into my eyes. I wanted to pull away, but it gave me a strange comfort, and I stayed there, close to him. He swayed my hand back and forth, and my heart went heavy.

"What happened?" I asked a mild choke brushed the back of my throat.

"Nothing! Why?" He asked, his eyes locking mine, making me nervous. He suddenly looked at me like a mature man. We stood in front of each other like never before, like grown-ups.

"I should leave! Happy birthday!" I hugged him. I could feel his restless breath. And he lingered on the hug. I could feel something more than just friendship there.

Back at home when I spoke with my sister about feeling something more than friendship toward Ashwin, she reacted as if it would be the eighth wonder in the world to fall for a man who was younger than me.

"Oh, come on Shama! He is younger than you! He's like your brother!" Her big eyes made me frame the thought that it was a sin to think of anything beyond friendship for Ashwin.

"I know!" I nodded, swallowing a lump at the back of my throat.

"What will your friends think? He is still in college, but you are out of college in a couple of months and will be working somewhere. What will you tell people… that your boyfriend is still an undergrad?" Her words sounded harsh but true to me.

"Come on, he's not my boyfriend!" I frowned.

"That's good! You'll find a perfect man for you; don't worry!" She walked to the kitchen, and I followed, my brain trying to flush all his thoughts.

Yes, he's just a good friend!

My senses commanded my heart. The following few days, his thoughts came many times, but I kept forcefully flushing them over and again.

The next month, we moved into a new house, closer to my sister's would-be in-laws' residence. Her marriage date got fixed, and we all got busy with that.

After moving home, I tried calling Ashwin's house number, but his mother said that he was gone to his grandparents in Ooty for the summer holidays. I hesitated to leave my new number or address with her, but I never called him after that. Meeting him and letting him know about my new address came to my mind many times, but somehow each time it got buried within my mind when I thought about my sister's advice on the absurdity of having a relationship with a younger man. "Ashwin Roy," the name remained in my memory as "once upon a time best friend."

Chapter 4

"A heck of a story! How can someone abruptly forget her best friend? Is it even possible?" Pallavi commented, bringing me back to the present. She merged onto Highway 5 and tuned the speed of the car higher than usual.

"I don't know!" I looked blankly at the series of Christmas lights decorated on both sides of the highway. I broke a piece from a graham cracker and shoved it in my mouth, giving an irked expression to Pallavi.

"Don't dirty the car, girl!" She said, and I pulled a face.

"Come on! I'm hungry!" I said, and she allowed me to eat two more pieces which melted my heart.

"You can be a sweetheart at times!" I kissed her closed fist, and she gave me an innocent smile which was otherwise unusual for her character.

"Btw, are you still going to Seattle tomorrow for your workshop on some philosophical muse or whatever? Pallavi never left a chance to willfully irritate me, talking strangely about my passion, poetry writing. She smirked.

I ignored her expression. "Yup! I am! Wanna join?" I asked her, knowing that even if it was the last thing left on earth, she would not join. Moreover, her family commitments were always more serious than my poetry passion.

“Is he coming?… I mean the charismatic man! Is he coming to the event?” She said with a wink. A funny smile brushed her lips.

“He’s supposed to… never heard from him for a long time though!” I felt thoughtful. A blush made a way to my lips, but I tried suppressing it, wishing not to give any further opportunity to Pallavi for pulling my leg talking about Shankar!”

“What was his name again? Umm… Satish… or… Sahil, the great poet?” Pallavi went on.

“Shankar…” My own voice echoed in my head.

“Oh yes! Shankar, the great poet!” Pallavi mouthed.

Our evening was a usual evening. Pallavi and I decided to spend the evening in a bar before heading back home.

We sat on the wooden bar stools and looked around the antique décor of the place. It had a cowboy concept involving leather and wood and dim lights. A few guitarists played soft rock on the dais at the corner of the big hall.

“Pick your poison!” I gestured to Pallavi, and she pointed to Macallan single malt.

We ordered two large whiskeys on rocks and cheered for a toast. “To your visit to the poetry event!” Pallavi shrieked. “Cheers!” We downed our drinks as a few men in the bar, maybe in their thirties, spared us steamy looks.

“Does Shankar know that you are going there?” Pallavi’s question startled me.

I nodded in denial.

There was always a soft corner in my heart for Shankar, and he was well aware of it.

Shankar SinghaRoy, my guide, my philosopher, my friend... I look up to him! My inner voice spoke again. His poems touched me each time I read them. The philosophical touch that's there in all his poems always made me thoughtful. A unique amalgamation of love, emotions, life, tragedy, and the almighty made each of his poems very special. When I met him for the first time at a small event in Chennai, I was in college, and he was in his late forties. He had a magical aura that always amazed me. I was going to see him after a decade and some change. Even though I kept in touch with him by calling him occasionally, I was too eager to meet him at the Seattle event. My mind filled with joy at the thought of meeting my idol.

That night, back at home, when I was packing my bags for the next day's travel, my phone rang out loud, but I disconnected the call upon seeing Samuel's name on the screen.

Following the call, a message popped up. "Please call! Don't stop talking to me like this! I can explain!"

What was he trying to make me understand or explain? Did he try to infer that hiding his marital status was just a mistake? If he was just looking for a one-night stand, then he could have very well gone to a different place and found a partner... bloody moron! Or was he calling for his gold ear stud that was still lying in my bag? Fucker!

My mind voice blurted out, and I bit my tongue, thinking if it was audible enough to wake up Pallavi. I opened my purse and saw Sam's glittering ear stud that he had asked me to keep safely when he lost the lock. It glistened under the yellow light of my bedroom, reminding me of our intimacy, reminding me of him at the nook of the restaurant, my lips gliding smoothly on his lips and the steamy romance... I snorted in disgust. I planned to throw that into the garbage first thing the following morning.

"Hope you had a wonderful day! Good night!" A message from Ashwin brought a smile to my face. But involving myself in another romantic relationship was not on my mind at all.

"Good night!" I typed and sent the message without lingering on the conversation. A waving emoticon flashed on the screen, and I smiled.

Another message from Samuel frustrated me enough that I decided to switch off my phone for the night.

My faith in love started to fade away, and I began to believe that all men I came across were the same and wanted exactly the same thing from me.

All bloody morons!

Seattle Book Event

I chose to wear a black and white off-shoulder semi-formal dress with minimal makeup and accessories. My shoulder-length wavy hair was left loose, and I styled them with my favorite curl cream, crunching them into tighter curls. I walked to the event to enjoy a session of a philosophical speech by Shankar... *my Shankar.*

Wearing a bright blue and yellow T-shirt on top of a pair of semi-formal pants, Shankar stood out in the huge crowd. He looked so different from the rest of the people present there. Most of them wore subtle combinations of clothing or stayed formal. He would be above sixty-five or so. Even though he looked older than last time, there was always an aura around him that separated him from the rest. His long beard, the tranquil expression on his face yet bright big eyes, a beautiful smile, and a tall structure were way beyond my words. He was sitting tall in the first row, and I sat in the fifth. The hall was full, and I wanted to talk to him desperately. When he was invited to join the other guests on the dais, he took a little longer to walk than usual. It looked to me like old age had started to lower his pace, but he still looked gorgeous. My heart literally skipped a beat, and I was in awe, staring at him throughout the program.

After the main program got over, I wanted to meet him. I walked to him after the crowd in the hall broke off.

"Hello, Sir! How are you? Do you remember me?" I reached out to shake hands with him, my face blushing.

"Hey, Shyama! How are you, young lady?" He smiled and embraced me in a soft hug. My body kind of melted in his gentle grip.

"I'm great! I was just waiting to talk to you!" I said, and he smiled, nodding.

We spoke for some time standing there and then decided to go to the nearby café for a quick coffee. He walked, and I followed. A smile lingered on my face, and so did his.

Coffee with Shankar

There was something beautiful about Shankar. I could see the aura that went about his face, as if I was getting engulfed in the depth of his knowledge each time he moved his lips to speak his words. His gray hair and beard, in contrast with the gleaming eyes full of charm and a calm face of wisdom, floored me each time I came across this scholar.

He took a sip from his double shot espresso, and I from my soya latte. We munched on some kettle-baked chips while I was trying to linger my time with him.

"So where are you put up here? In a hotel?" He asked, checking the time on the huge antique wall clock kept at the nook of the café.

"Yes, it's not that far, though," I replied with a blush that made him smile.

"I've written a poem for you!" I said, handing over a piece of paper to Shankar.

"Sure! A poem?" he asked, and I nodded.

"This definitely interests me. Let me see what you have got for me." His gesture made me a bit nervous. *What if he didn't like my poem? What if he thought I was going overboard with my emotions for him? What if...?*

A series of thoughts whisked through my brain like a whirlpool while he was reading my poem. His lips cracked into smiles in between reading, and I bit my lips. His occasional glance at me made me conscious, but I still managed to hold up and sat poised, looking at him, admiring him, feeling my respect for him... or maybe it was *love!*

I named my poem "The Spiritual Aura." I was longing to share it with Shankar, and finally, it was the day.

He read it softly, occasionally sipping his coffee, and I kept admiring him.

My fingers clutched in nervousness, but yet they wanted to touch him to see if he was real…

The poem went like this:

In a gathering of enlightened souls
When I first saw him
Walking in an easy gait
With a charming smile that emitted an eternal grace
My eyes went craving way beyond my sway
Seeking to have another glance

A seraphic aura went about his face
Its beaming rays must be enchanted with its own luster
And his smile weaving a divine maze
His words left a soothing timbre
Rendering a serene peace
The command of his voice calm yet so strong
Hearing that any pain could ease
My heart melted and halted standing at the nook
Struck by his aura that vaulted the barrier of his face stark

His white beard coordinated with his gray hair
The twinkle of his eyes captivated all the living souls present there
He stood in a vibrant blue attire
And my heart churned in delight
When I walked up to him
With an amazed mind and a mild fear

When I reached to shake his hand
His tranquil gaze flashed a soothing smile
A vibe of spirituality broke into my vein
Soaking my mind in a divine notion

I sought to muster the courage
To converse with this scholar I met
I stood numb facing the ocean of knowledge
Or the mountain of literature
My words faltered
Thinking how to match up the pace
But he spoke with such ease
Rendering an instant comfort indeed

I sat beside him
On the wooden bench prim
Admiring the beautiful soul
And the tufts of his hair that needed a slight trim
When he skimmed through poems few
He maybe clueless but his magnetic aura bounded over the brim

His graceful age
His divine self
His peaceful presence
His ocean-deep knowledge
His beautiful smile
His twinkling eyes
His talk on literature
His content soul yet with a thirst for learning more
They whisked my mind
Like a weak leaf amazed and seized by a whirlwind wild

I feel like a drop of water in front his eternal ocean
But I still craved to stay around
Falling too hard into his allure and passion
I long to see him again
Wishing hard to sense the aura divine
Praying for a moment of our meet again
Looking to solicit a dash of his spiritual shine

If love is the synonym of respect
And admiring his charm is the meaning of life
Then can I not say that I love him to the moon and back
Seeking to be enlightened by his enriched spiritual knack

"It's a beautiful poem, I must say!" he said, and I bit my lips yet again.

"Thank you so much! I couldn't be happier that you've liked it!" I tried to look into his eyes, but they were so strong and full of wisdom that I felt very small in front of those eyes.

"You know, I have a grandson who would be almost your age!" His words hurt me and brought me back to reality. I nodded, still smiling.

"I've got a picture for you. Do you wanna see that?" I asked, acknowledging the grandson's theory.

"Sure! I'd love to see!"

I handed over a printout that had an image of Shankar and me. I had managed to click a picture the previous time I met him and developed the photo so that I could show it to him. He appreciated my gesture. The rest of the evening went beautifully by his side, talking about life's philosophy, the ultimate power and beyond, poetry, and travel. He spoke about India's ancient mythologies and modern science, and I listened to him like how a follower would listen to his or her Guru.

Shankar knew that I was weak for him. He knew I had strong feelings toward him. He knew my respect and love for him, but he didn't want to encourage that. Probably the age gap between us gave him a fright. He didn't live with his wife, but maybe he loved to be a loner till the end, enjoying the solitude of life.

A message popped up on my phone. "Hey, I'm moving to Kolkata! Are you coming to Kolkata anytime soon?" It was from Ashwin.

I wondered why he would move to Kolkata as I knew that his family belonged to Chennai, and he was raised there too.

"Great news! I'll try to meet you next time when I visit Kolkata." I replied. Shankar seemed busy reading a book. My glance drifted to him, but he didn't notice that.

"When are you coming?" Another message from Ashwin.

"Maybe next year!" I replied. A mild swallow choked in the back of my throat fearing his frequent messages. I was determined not to get into any more relationships save for Shankar. Shankar held an absolutely special place in my heart.

Chapter 5

Six months later:
Kolkata: The City of Joy

I think I deserved to take a break after roasting myself for three non-vacation years in my nine-to-five technical job. It was my less decision and more obsession to pursue a career in creative writing and eventually took a short crash course on the same. Those days, my aunt used to live near Calcutta University, and hence I planned to stay there for a couple of months, spending my savings on learning the ins and outs of creative writing. My mother had a mixed reaction, but my father was extremely happy as their daughter was finally back from abroad. My apparent purpose was the course, but at the same time, I wished to meet Shankar who lived only an hour away from my place, in the same town. Even Ashwin lived in the same town, but my interest was more toward Shankar and not Ashwin. Like the long-gone college days, Ashwin remained a 'dude' friend.

I had been to Shankar's house quite a couple of times, but he kept himself reserved, choosing not to discuss anything about my love or emotions toward him. His indirect rejection was wearing me down, and one fine day I decided to open up to him, frankly, deeply, madly, helplessly about what I really felt for him.

Even that day, at the break of dawn, I dreamed about Shankar and me. I dreamed that we were at my breakfast table having a philosophical discussion over a cup of coffee. His eyes were intensely on me, and I admired him madly. His fingers brushed through my hand while explaining the connection between the heart and the soul. I clutched his fingers, interlacing them into mine. I took his hand and rubbed our clutched hands on my cheek. Our eyes locked, and we kissed deeply. I could feel his breath. It was calm as if there was no rush anywhere. We kept kissing, exploring the taste of our mouths. My breathing went high in sleep and a sudden rush in my hormones made me warm. When I woke up, my body was sweaty. I loved my moist body.

A beeping sound from my phone grabbed my attention.

It was a message from Ashwin. He messaged me the other day too. I wanted to respond to him, but something stopped me from doing that. I did not want to take his interest very seriously. The reason could be my past breakups or the reason could be Shankar, however, I was trying to stay away from Ashwin. Shankar was different, and he in no way fell into the category of those useless untrustworthy men. Maybe that's why I believed him, and I loved him and wanted to pursue him.

"Hey, wanna catch up? I am near your house around 7 pm. How about a coffee at the Coffee house?" A delightful message from Ashwin made me smile. I was on the way to Shankar's house.

"Let's see. I will try!" I responded.

“Really? See you then!” He sounded excited, and I was still thinking about how to bring up my intimate topic to Shankar.

3 PM at Shankar’s house:

“Shama, do you want a cup of tea? Kakoli is making tea and snacks.” Kakoli, his maid and cook, was in her fifties, and Shankar loved her like his own daughter.

“Sure, Sir! I would love to!” I said and dropped my bag in the corner, opening one mythological book. We were supposed to talk about the Upanishads that day. He chanted mantras in his bass voice in between the learning sessions, and I was waiting for a chance to talk about my emotions to him. I listened to his chanting but might be with less attention than on other days, and he could very well figure that out.

Kakoli came and kept the two cups of tea and one plate full of ‘pakoda’ in front of us. She grinned and looked at Shankar.

Damn! Everybody loves him!

My inner voice echoed. I smiled at her, but my core cursed heavily.

We took a break from sipping our tea and consuming the snacks.

“You look lost, Shama!” he asked seeing me gazing out the window. The beautiful mango tree in the yard swayed its branches.

“Sir, I wanna say something!” I said, humble, gazed down, still, and hoping to get a positive answer.

"Not again, Shama! We spoke about it, and I told you clearly that I'm not up for any relationship! I have crossed that age and energy; now I look at life altogether in a different perspective!" His face glared wise with a composed expression.

"But I love you! I feel the urge to be with you every single day!" My voice shook. He patted my back.

"It's normal to feel this way at your age, and I don't blame you! It's just an attraction! You will find the right person for you!" He walked to the window and looked out. The mild drizzle gave a perfect smell of petrichor.

Kakoli finished the household chores and slammed the door shut with a creaking sound on her way out.

I kept silent. A message popped on the screen.

"Is the plan still on?" The message read, Ashwin.

"Yes, see you!" I replied, waiting to hear more from Shankar.

"There are so many couples in the world with huge age differences! We might become just another example!" My voice pitched a little high understanding that it was only Shankar and me in the room.

"I don't think anyone ever thought of this big of an age difference! I am sixty-eight, Shama!" He walked back to the reading nook, and I bit my lips.

"You are doing great in creative writing, in philosophy. Keep up your good works!" He said.

"Thanks!" My gaze down.

"Can I kiss you?" It just slipped out of my tongue, and he laughed out loud.

"Are you serious? Don't burden your brain so much!" He closed the book indirectly calling it a day. I blushed and got to my feet and walked to the door.

He was not irritated or offended by my proposal to kiss him, but he didn't kiss me either, and I didn't have the courage to go closer to him.

He sent me off. It was about to be 7 PM, and I walked in the direction of the coffee day.

Meeting with Ashwin Roy:

I saw a man in a long white self-designed kurta and a pair of blue jeans standing across the road toward the end of the lane. When I approached closer, he walked toward me. There was a strange surprise on his face, a gleam of sheer happiness, and a pure broad smile. He looked much different than last time when I last saw him. He looked taller now, broader, and composed. His curly hair was shortened to a much shorter hairstyle, and he kept stubbles which gave him a raw look, very earthy, unique, handsome, and sexy to be precise.

"Hey!" He pulled me into a tight embrace. "Is this really you?" I felt his heart thumping harder against my chest.

"Yup!" I blushed ear to ear. He kept his fingers clutched in my fingers for a couple of seconds before letting them off. There was a familiar warmth in him that felt so comforting.

"See… I'm getting goosebumps!" He rubbed his arm. I smiled, "why?"

He narrowed his eyes, and I nodded in assertion. We both blushed suddenly.

“Let’s go to the coffee shop!” I proposed.

“After you!” He ushered me the way.

We chugged up the steep stairs and entered the famous India Coffee Day, taking a seat at one of the tables. On the way, I grabbed a book from the stall beneath Coffee Day, and Ashwin stared at it with a frown. “Don’t worry; I’m not reading it now!” He smiled a witty smile. A waiter dressed in white and red walked to our table with a menu card in his hand, and took our order for coffee and bread omelets.

“So, finally, we are meeting!” He sighed deeply. I gave a quick rub to his hand. “Yes.”

“And I’m really sorry for absconding all of a sudden! I never intended to do so, though!” It was a long-pending apology. The realization of not saying goodbye came much later, and by then, both time and distance had come between us.

“Seventeen years and three months!” He sighed.

“Wow! You are keeping track of it!” I was shocked, thinking of his memory power.

“Of course! I could never forget you!” His eyes darkened, making me embarrassed.

“Oh, Ashwin! I’m really sorry for vanishing like that!” I gave his hand a friendly rub again. But he held my hand this time.

“I want to confess something.” He seemed thoughtful, probably trying to gather the correct words.

“Confess! What is it?” My eyes were on him.

“I came to your house later…” He said in an unfinished way. “…with flowers and gifts… to propose to you!” His voice shook. And my core trembled.

“What?” I looked into his intense gaze.

“Yes, seventeen years back…” he sighed.

“Come on, Shama… even on my birthday… You know… we were about to kiss!” He said, his voice strong, and my body shivered. My gaze went to the water-filled glass where I could see the reflection of his face. I did remember it, and I also remembered talking to my sister after that when my sister reminded me of his age.

“You are younger than me! I thought it was not normal to kiss a man who’s younger…” My voice was more like a murmur.

“I am sorry!” I pursed my lips.

He smiled.

The same waiter came back with two mugs of coffee and omelets. They looked authentic and smelled heavenly. We got busy mixing sugar into the coffee and pepper into the eggs.

He didn’t respond to my sorry. We had the rest of the coffee in silence, and then he dropped me home on his way back.

Too many things clogged my mind post that day. The person whom I loved considered me like his grandkid, and the person who loved me madly was not able to find a place in my heart because I was older than him, and the two people with whom I made love wanted only the physical part of mine. My life felt like a puzzle to me where all the pieces werc present but connected wrongly.

Should I try talking to Shankar again on the same thing? Why is Ashwin still loving me so much even after we were disconnected?

Thoughts bothered me, but I had to go to the airport the next day morning to pick up Pallavi. She was visiting me for a couple of days.

Chapter 6

At the airport:

Pallavi exited the airport as I recognized her favorite bright yellow maxi dress. Her hair was tied into a ponytail, and she managed to look fresh even after the long journey. Ashwin wanted to tag along, so he joined me on the way to the airport. Pallavi came rushing and wrapped me tight, pulling me into a warm hug. Ashwin felt a little out of place; so, he looked around.

"Hi Pallavi, this is Ashwin, my college friend! And Ashwin, this is Pallavi, my colleague and also my best friend!" I introduced them to each other. Ashwin welcomed her with a brief hug and with a small bouquet. He insisted on carrying her stroller, and hence Pallavi handed that over to Ashwin. We both walked a little ahead of Ashwin, and he followed us, giving us the room to do some girly talk.

"He's handsome!" Pallavi winked, and I eyed her. "I know, but we can talk about it later. Moreover, he's just a friend!" She pulled a face, and I smiled walking toward the call taxi counter. An old man sat there with a grumpy face. It felt to us as if we had woken him up from a deep slumber.

"Did he come all the way from the other end of the city just to give you company to the airport?" Pallavi's next query.

“Kind of!” I smiled, thinking about Ashwin’s caring nature. I had never thought that before.

“What are friends for, then?” I said, still hanging on to the friendship factor.

“He likes you, girl! But you don’t seem to buy it!” Pallavi opened her wallet, but all she had were dollars.

“Let me pay!” I handed over the cash, and we took the token. “No way! He’s just a friend… I love Shankar!” I said in a subdued voice while further looking for Ashwin. He got involved talking to some known person at the corner of a coffee shop.

“You are in love with him too!” Pallavi saw me looking at Ashwin. “Else why would your eyes drift toward him every now and then?”

“Bullshit!” I walked faster in the direction of the rented car hub, and Pallavi waved at Ashwin, showing him the nook of the taxi stand.

We reached the hotel, and Pallavi checked in. We waited in the lobby and then finally got a room. Pallavi freshened up, and we ordered food and drinks in the room itself. After having dinner, Ashwin made drinks for all three of us, and we got involved in a binge chat until dawn.

Pallavi had a habit of getting too close to men. Even though she was happily married, I had always noticed her flirting side. So her usual flirting continued even here, even with Ashwin. And it seemed like alcohol had taken over the whole thing to a different level altogether.

“How come you don’t have a girlfriend?” She started with her favorite topic, ‘romance’.

"I did have a girlfriend, but things didn't work out between us," he said politely, making another round of drinks for us.

"What things?" she sounded cheeky, and I rolled my eyes.

Pallavi tugged onto his elbow, fawning over Ashwin every now and then while sipping her whiskey. Even though I wasn't in love with Ashwin, something was uneasy inside my heart, and I tried to overlook their closeness and play something on the TV. Without my knowledge, I drifted off to sleep while Ashwin and Pallavi's chatting noises came into my eardrums on and off.

A bad dream of Ashwin and Pallavi making out woke me up at the creak of dawn. I looked around and saw them sleeping, sharing the same pillow. Their faces faced each other as if they had just broken off a deep kiss. Did they really kiss or was it just a nightmare? Some sadness choked in the back of my throat. I decided to get up and go to the balcony for some fresh air. At the night table, I found the cigarette pack and a lighter. It was probably Ashwin's. I clutched them and tiptoed my way to the balcony.

Why was I even thinking of Ashwin! Was I too desperate for love…?

I took a few puffs of smoke and exhaled in the air with a sigh. The morning sun was yet to rise, and the sky looked gorgeously beautiful in an orange tone. Another smoke and I felt a little bit lightheaded. A few slum kids passing by looked at me in a strange way and giggled. I waved at them as they vanished out of my sight.

The beautiful sky and a sad state of mind over smoke in hand felt relaxing when a voice traveled from my back reaching my ears.

"Hey, what you doing here?" Ashwin joined me on the balcony. His face appeared drowsy, and his hair was unkempt. His stark features had manly warmth in them. He no longer looked like the little guy; no more did the timid look daunt his face.

"Waiting to see the sunrise!" I offered him a cigarette, and he pulled one from the packet. I lit the smoke poised between his fingers. He took a puff and looked at the sky and then at me.

"Do you know something?" He looked into my eyes, his gaze strong.

I looked at him, smiling, nodding.

"I still have the gifts that I once got for you! The dry flowers, the letters, the cards, everything! I searched for you almost every day, in every nook of the city, wishing to find you desperately!" His gaze darkened. "Did I offend you so much that you left me without even meeting me once?" His question didn't get an answer. My guilty face looked down thoughtfully. "I didn't want to get into a love relationship so early, Ashwin!" I looked at him. He placed his smoke on the wooden rail and pulled me into a warm grip. My nose almost touched his nose.

"Do you know what love is?" he asked. I froze in his arms due to nervousness.

"What I have for you is love! The state of my mind when you are close to me is love! Waiting for only you all these years uncertainly is love! Even knowing that you have a soft corner for the old man who's not even bothered for you is love! "Do you realize it?" His grip tightened; I suddenly felt small, buried in his broad chest. His long fingers brushed my cheeks. He touched my lips. My core clenched, feeling the touch of his skin, as if his warm touch was melting my body, inviting me into a deep intimacy.

He clutched the collar of my night dress softly and pulled me into a kiss. We kissed again and again, my mouth exploring the warmth of his mouth, my breaths paced up, and his breaths were louder than mine. With a thumping heart, we kissed, hugged, moaned. Our grips went tighter, and our bodies became sweaty. We slowly walked into the room and then moved into the bathroom. Pallavi slept like a small baby, leaving a soft snore sound. I closed the door, locking us into the solitude of the small bathroom. I moaned deeply when Ashwin made love to me. Our clothes fell on the floor, and our exposed bodies stood against each other, feeling each other's snuggles. A soft cry escaped from my mouth for every stroke of his love, with every passionate kiss he planted on my body, with every magic his fingers made on me. We loved each other till the end of our strength and finally lay flat on the small rug of the bathroom. I could see so much love in Ashwin's eyes for me on that day, in that moment.

"Hey, we just made love!" he kissed my shoulder. A knock on the door flinched us out. Pallavi was standing on the other side of the door. I bit my tongue. I shoved myself into my top and night pants and opened the door.

"Hey, you got a call!" She handed over the phone to me and looked at both of us with a smirk.

"What's cooking?" she raised her eyebrow with a mischievous smile. Ashwin walked out quietly, embarrassed. His hair was messed up. Seeing us, it was not very difficult for Pallavi to find out what was happening behind the closed bathroom door.

"Hello!" I called back to the same number.

"I am Kakoli, Sir is in the hospital! Can you come to see him, please?" Kakoli, Shankar's maid, sounded panicked and frightened.

"What? I am coming!" I adjusted my dress, lifted my bag and rushed to the exit to the main road to get a taxi to the hospital.

"What happened?" A chorus came from both Ashwin and Pallavi.

"Shankar…" I stared at Pallavi.

Chapter 7

A moderately dim light, blue bedsheet and an adjustable bed surrounded by different types of machines that were taking his vitals and a white warm sheet covered up to his chest, Shankar appeared smaller than usual. As if a sudden sickness has taken ten more years from his life. Multiple wires were glued on different parts of his body. The oxygen mask on his face looked brand new. The hospital room had a fresh fragrance of linen unlike the usual floor cleaning disinfectants like most of the clinics.

I walked closer, and the nurse gave me a darting look, scanning me from top to bottom. She stopped me. A safety apron was given to them before going any closer to him. Hence I went back and walked to one of the common changing rooms toward the end of the corridor.

The apron felt like a crisp layer of blotting paper.

"How's he doing now?" I asked the nurse, concerned.

"Less critical than the time when he was brought in! Are you his daughter?" She asked, checking the level on the saline bag and taking a fresh bag from the bottom drawer of one of the side tables.

"No!" my throat almost choked hearing the daughter word. "His friend," I said, and she gave me a strange look. I ignored her expressions.

"Is he awake? Can I talk to him?" I asked, resting my fingers next to his pillow. His glowing face looked pale, and his gray hair looked whiter, but he still looked handsome to me. He was holding something in his hand, between his fingers. It looked like a hard copy of an image. His eyelids fluttered as if he was able to sense that someone was around.

"Only five minutes!" The nurse walked away to the other nook of the huge room where another critical patient was resting. The room felt cold as I moved the blanket from his chest to his neck.

"Shankar Sir!" I stroked my fingers along his hair. He nodded a very weak nod.

"How are you feeling?" I asked, and he nodded again. His eyelids fluttered a little.

The photo resting on his chest was not in his grip anymore, so I took it to check. It was a photo of a beautiful woman, an English woman. Or maybe European. She looked very pretty in a gown and braided hair. The picture was black and white, and her attire looked old-fashioned, like some traditional western wear, probably people wore back in the sixties.

Who's she?

My mind's voice echoed. *And what's the image doing here in the hospital? Could this be the reason for his sudden attack?*

The doctor breezed in, and the door behind him creaked to closure. His white coat sailed in the same sway of his manly walk, and he stopped next to the bed.

"Hello, doctor!" I smiled.

"He's doing much better now! Are you his daughter?" The same question came across.

"No… I'm from his close circle; my name is Shama."

"Hello Shama." A short greeting from his side, and then he got busy looking into his vitals.

"Umm… what exactly happened?" I asked him. My eyes were still glued to the photo.

"He had a massive attack. Actually, there were two attacks, one minor and another pretty major. By the way, do you know anyone from his family?" He asked, checking his pulse.

"Not really!"

He never said anything about his family, and I never asked either.

A deep sigh. And the Doctor walked around the bed to check his folder that was kept on his night table.

"Then how to find his relatives?" I asked, curious!

Is the European lady his wife or ex-wife or something?

I scanned through the blurred image again.

"Don't worry, it might take a little time, but we will have to get hold of someone from his relatives. Nice to meet you!" he exited the room, and the nurse stared at me, reminding me of the five-minute meeting window.

"Can I come to see him tomorrow? What about his food?" I asked her.

"After 6 pm, and no outside food is allowed at this moment!" she said with a straight face.

"Hmm..." I looked at Shankar. He was sleeping like a newborn. I kept the photo back on his chest and made his left hand rest on that and left the room. My eyes welled up once I was out. I loved him so much and I couldn't see him in that condition.

My phone vibrated in my tote bag, and I fished out to see who it was.

Pallavi!

"Hi..." I picked up the call. My voice sounded low, and she knew about my attachment to Shankar.

"I'm sorry Shama, but to be honest, we could kind of foresee it... isn't it?" she said.

"Foresee what?" I mumbled.

"I mean, he stayed alone with no close relatives around him. And he is in his seventies for Christ's sake! It's normal to fall sick now!" her voice came broken as if she was walking on a busy road and talking to me.

"Not seventies!" I frowned.

"Whatever! Hey, I forgot to tell you something! Something Nice!" she said, back to her bubbly voice.

"What is it?"

"I bumped into Sam and his wife at the airport while coming to India, and guess what I did?" She said, excited.

"Sam? You mean Samuel Jacob? What was he doing at the airport?" I brows furrowed.

"Yes, the same Samuel. And I handed his wife one of my ear studs that looked pretty similar to his lost one and told her that her husband was hitting on every other woman in his office! You should have just seen her face, dear!" Pallavi burst into a huge laughter probably scaring some pedestrians out there.

Fuck!

"Really?" I smiled. A sudden peace brushed my mind.

"I'm proud of you! See you soon!" I hung up.

Back in Pallavi's room:

Pallavi made green tea for the three of us, and we prepared to spend the night watching a horror film.

Pallavi was aware of the love factor that started brewing between Ashwin and me still she did not hesitate to sit between us. A strange glance was exchanged between us. We watched about half the film when Pallavi got a call from her husband. I paused the television, and she walked to the balcony with her headphones in her ear.

"How's he doing now?" Ashwin asked me. His fingers brushed my fingers. I pulled away softly.

"He's still unconscious!" I said thoughtfully.

"Hey!" he pulled me close looking into my eyes.

I smiled. The memories of the previous night flashed in front of my eyes and gave me a hint of blush.

"Don't pull away… I wanna grow old with you! You have no idea how much I'm falling for you!" Ashwin cupped my face, but my mind still thought about the image that Shankar was holding.

I could see pure love in Ashwin's intense gaze, but my eyes were still occupied, and my mind wandered elsewhere.

"What happened?" he said, and I smiled, feeling a bit embarrassed.

"Shankar was holding someone's photo…" My unfinished sentence made him irked. His hands curled in crossing in front of his chest.

"I'm sorry!" I murmured, but Ashwin walked out of the room.

"See you tomorrow." He closed the door on the way out. I sullen my face, and Pallavi walked in, clueless about what was happening.

Next day in the hospital:

Ashwin dropped me at the entrance of the hospital as I walked in, and his eyes trailed me. I looked at him and smiled, but his smile didn't reach his eyes. It seemed like he was still disturbed by my previous night's cold response. But I was happy that he still came to meet me that morning. I loved him too, but I needed time to find more about the picture that Shankar was holding.

When I walked into the room, another lady was sitting by Shankar's bed. She seemed to be of the same age, might be a bit younger than him.

"Hello!" I said, and she smiled at me, nodding.

Shankar's eyes were half opened, and he didn't use the oxygen mask anymore. His face looked a little brighter than last time. The photo that I saw last time was on the night table then, flipped over.

"Sir!" I said.

He looked at me, but there was no smile on his face, as if he was looking at some stranger.

"It's me… Shama!" I said, feeling a tweak of pain inside my chest.

"Do I know you?" he mumbled, and that came like a sheer shock to me.

A quick glance got exchanged between the lady next to his bed and me. "Some memories are gone… but he still remembers the past. Only the recent past got affected." The lady said when Shankar stared at her.

"Water… Bakula!" Shankar murmured.

Bakula! Who is Bakula? His wife?

I couldn't stay there anymore. It was breaking my heart. On the way back to the entrance, the lady came out of the room to send me off.

"I know he doesn't recognize you. I'm really sorry!" she clutched my fingers in a tight grip.

"And you?" I mastered the courage to ask it finally.

"His ex-wife, Bakula." She responded in a calm tone.

An empty feeling brushed the core of my being.

"Ok… can I ask you something?"

"Sure!" she looked so serene and immaculate in her white and pink saree.

"Whose photo was that?"

Few seconds of silence hovered us making the void air hush.

"Anesthesia! He loved her… loved her so much! Their love was the reason behind our separation… it was so obvious that I had to walk away." The unfinished reply punched me a blow.

"Anesthesia passed away few days back and the news of her death gave him the attack!" her voice rustled in my ear making echoes and I stood helplessly but without any outward reaction.

"I am sorry! I need to leave!" I hurried up, hiding the tears at the brim of my eyes.

When I came out of the hospital, I saw Ashwin still waiting for me at the corner of the main gate. His face glowed just by getting a glance of mine. I could see his soul talking to me, telling that how much he longed for me, how much he loved me.

Maybe that's why people say we should love the person who loves you and not whom you love!

I kissed him under the dim light of the street. It felt like the perfect thing in the whole world.

He embraced me in his arms. My tears felt unstoppable, but there was an unknown tranquility in the air, so as in my soul.

Second Story: A Piece of Cake

Chapter 1

After handing a hundred rupee note to the blurred-eyed ailing auto-rickshaw driver, she thought whether to offer her sunglasses to him. But then a sudden change of mind stopped her, and she shoved that back into her tote. Her kohl-rimmed glance went to the rearview mirror where she caught a pair of lustful eyes darting at her. Fuck you… Moron!

She mouthed. Her fingers went to adjust her cotton mask that was color coordinating with her pants. The raising hormones of a few creatures seated under the shade of a huge banyan tree were obvious to the most. She spared a vexed look at them, and their gaped mouths closed instantly.

She got off the auto carefully, avoiding much skin contact with the door. She observed the pale green face mask of the auto driver that almost served no purpose as she scanned through the back seat one last time.

Two men in uniform and light blue surgical masks from the security office located at the front gate of the building walked toward her. One of them flaunted a courteous smile, "Welcome, Madam, I am the manager here!" He gave her a hand for moving four small yet heavy suitcases that she had with her. The other person, a young boy not in security uniform but looked more like a school uniform, followed the older man and carried the rest of her luggage. He appeared somewhere between a trainee security guard and just a poor boy serving them for a little tip.

"Abha Shanyal, moving to Wing A 1105! Bring the keys..." One of the guards hollered to the gatekeepers.

Should it be this public? She thought.

The auto-rickshaw that pulled over to drop her finally moved from the entrance when a fancy car sharply turned at the exit gate to merge onto the main road. The man behind the wheel, dressed up in a neat tuxedo, had his beard way too neatly trimmed and looked like a rapper except for a heavy gold chain around his neck. His spiked up gelled hair shone bright under the setting sun, and he spared a typical masculine look at Abha. She rolled her eyes. The lady sat next to him, seemed to be his better half, looked at her husband with narrowed eyes, and the tiny little kid waved at Abha, smiling. The situation threw her into a snigger. The wife mouthed something, and the man instantly moved his vision back onto the road. His gold-rimmed fancy glasses looked brand new. Abha stifled her laugh. Her white tank top, army green cotton stole matching with green loose-fitting pants, and short curly hair and tattooed right sleeve looked unique and attractive to the rest of the crowd of her new apartment.

"How was your journey, ma'am? I heard that the flights aren't safe yet!" The manager asked. His voice was more like a front desk receptionist of any hotel, clear speech, polite, rarely expected from a security guard of an apartment building.

Abha smiled. "Yes, but they have started following a good hygiene system." Her eyes scanned around the parking lot as they walked to the elevator corridor.

"Sure, Ma'am! This virus is taking a toll on everyone!" His eyes spared a quick glance at Abha's slender arms. The other boy, followed them with her suitcases, mostly had his gaze on the floor.

Her toned body, defined muscles, and kohl-bordered eyes, sharp nose and black nose ring looked sexy to her own self when she looked at herself at the full-size mirror inside the elevator. A smile cracked in when she checked out her sharp jawline. She adjusted her mask back on her face. The manager admired her on and off from the corner of his eyes whereas the younger one fixed his gaze to the elevator floor until the eleventh floor arrived.

"The intercom number for maintenance is 24 and 25 and for security, it is 16 or 17 for gate one and gate two. Please do call us if you need any kind of help. Plumber, carpenter, cleaners etc., pretty much anything!" Said the manager like a by hearted statement. Abha didn't fail to notice his mischievous smile.

"Sure. Thanks!" He handed over the keys, and Abha unlocked the jammed and rusty door. "Is this a very old society?" She asked seeing the condition of the lock. "You can say that! It's one of the oldest in this area." He gestured the boy to leave after he placed the suitcases at her doorstep. He moved a couple of steps back but didn't leave. "What's your name?" Abha asked the boy while her fingertips brushed the door surface checking the dirt level. She took a quick peek at his naïve look.

"Ram." A brief answer came from the shy teenager.

"And yes…cleaners for sure!" She looked at the manager, smiling, showing the amount of dirt that smudged her finger from the door.

"Sure, Ma'am! I'll send them right away. By the way, my name is Satish Jha! If you need anything else, please let me know." The manager said with a grin as he helped her drag the suitcases into the living room.

"Sure… it was wonderful meeting you!" Abha wondered what if he was not the manager there and what if she met him somewhere else. His eyes shone bright with life, and the brows bridged in the middle by a narrow hairy line. He daunted a handsome look.

"Hope you have a good stay! And I'm just a call away!" His words sounded a little flirtatious as he shook hand with Abha.

"Definitely!"

The younger one, who seemed to be below eighteen, followed the manager obediently as they both walked to the elevator.

Abha Shanyal, a freelance photographer working on street photography, got associated with one of the weekly journals. Their main office was based out of Delhi. And hence she moved from Mumbai to Delhi. Working for the new magazine, that too in a remote setup, was getting a bit challenging for her. Her boyfriend, Animesh, tried convincing her several times to stay back and also shared his interest in marrying Abha, but she wanted to try more career opportunities before settling down in life.

Dragging the suitcases to one corner of the hall, she turned on the ceiling fan and then slumped into the blue couch. She dragged one of the pillows to her lap and rested her elbows on it. Her nerves, achy from the hectic journey, demanded a hot shower and a long lie-in. She looked around and sighed, feeling lonely.

Abha made a perfect tenant for that furnished two BHK flat rented out by Mr. and Mrs. Dheeraj Patel who met her only once, that too virtually, over a video call. Her friend Kushi came over to see the house in person on behalf of Abha, though.

After a quick relaxation, she walked around to check the rooms and the bathrooms. Everything looked neat and well-maintained except the door and the lock. Two huge bedrooms with an open balcony, old style, with two full baths and a beautifully decorated kitchen looked perfect to her eyes. The view from the balcony gave a little disappointment since her previous house had an ocean view unlike this one. She looked over and saw a few kids playing in the park downstairs while a few ladies, apparently looked to be their guardians, sat on the benches chatting away the boring afternoon hours. She walked back to the kitchen. Except food, everything was available in the house including utensils and towels. Abha felt a bit peckish, and the huge nutty chocolate bar that Animesh gave her while sending her off came in handy. She smiled at it and took a big bite from it, settling down on the balcony chair, peering at the strip of the shops that looked like a cluster of matchboxes from the top.

The wooden easy chair at the balcony with cane-woven sitting base appeared great with the hanging old-fashioned bulb shade. It gave her an instant idea for a good photo. *The background of high-rise buildings can fade away with the total focus on the lamp and partly on the chair!* Abha's mind already pictured the end product of the photoshoot, but she felt too lazy to get on her feet and do the experiment. Instead, settling into the easy chair, she closed her eyes, and the thoughts of leaving her beloved and their common friends flashed one by one from her memory stack. She dozed off in no time with the chocolate bar in her hand resting on the high of her chest.

Time showed 8 PM on the rusted table clock, which probably was abandoned by the previous tenant. The rusted steel edge and the combination of light aqua of the clock looked uniquely antique to Abha. Her lazy eyes fluttered. Dusk turned duskier with more vehicle sounds drifting in the air, proclaiming the peak evening traffic. A voice of a kid, girlish, reading something, which sounded almost like chanting, seeped through Abha's ears waking her from her unplanned afternoon nap. The voice sounded innocent, soothing, and rhythmic. Abha looked around widely, opening the shutters of her eyes. A little of her chocolate got stuck to her T-shirt, and a few mosquitoes flew about her slender dusky leg attempting to draw some blood from her.

Come on, Abha!

She briskly got on her feet, batting away the mosquitoes, and made her way to the kitchen. The reading sound came louder when another kid joined, making that a chorus read, and Abha closed the mesh of the balcony door to keep the mosquitoes away. She gulped down a glass full of water and was about to maneuver through the suitcases and boxes on the way to the bathroom when the doorbell rang out aloud, tripping her almost to the floor.

Ouch!

Abha rubbed her mildly bruised ankle and limped her way to the door to attend the door when the bell rang again, giving her a freaking jitter.

"Who's that?" She said hastily while her brows cringed out of pain she just received from her four-wheel suitcase.

A middle-aged lady with neatly combed hair, a huge red dot on the forehead, and a faded red and yellow saree grinned broadly.

"Madam, I heard that you have moved in today. You must be looking for a maid! If you want, I can come from tomorrow morning." Her smile went broader, and her bangles jiggled, making a beautiful echo in the confined corridor.

"How do you know that I have just moved in today?" Abha asked, surprised. Her white sleeveless top and army green stole looked attractive to the vegetable shop delivery boy who came to deliver veggies to the neighbor's house. Instead of ringing their doorbell, he stood frozen there, staring at Abha and listened to their conversation. He was hardly around ten to twelve years, and hence Abha didn't bother much about him being there or observing them.

"What are you watching? Wait… let me tell your manager!" The maid yelled, eyeballing the boy, and he scurried back to the staircase after dropping the vegetable-filled bag at their doorstep.

She grinned at Abha once again, "He works at the grocery store downstairs… Golu, his name is."

Abha nodded.

"The security uncle told me that a new madam rented this flat… so I came by to ask you if you needed a maid. I can come from tomorrow if you want." She repeated.

"Security? Satish?" Abha looked for a towel to clean the door. The lady followed her and entered the living room. "Not Satish Sir. Niranjan." Her grin claimed that she had maintained a good relation with the people working at the gate. But Abha cared less as it didn't matter to her anyways.

"Madam, don't worry, I'll clean this door first thing tomorrow morning!" Her statement stopped Abha from rubbing the good towel on the door.

"Can you buy a good broomstick, a couple of kitchen towels, and a mop stick tomorrow morning?" Abha asked, throwing the towel on the couch.

She nodded cheerfully.

"Are you a good cook? I need someone who can cook and do all my housework, and my budget is not more than five thousand a month." Abha sat down feeling tired.

"I can ask my niece, Priya. Please give us an extra 200 rupees for commute. I'll keep your house neat and tidy, and she can cook. Ask anyone about my work! Ask the 7th-floor aunty; she will tell you about my cleanliness!" She kept bragging about her work when Abha felt a little churn in her stomach.

"Ok… come from tomorrow morning. Btw, what's your name?" she asked the lady while closing the door.

"Shushila. I'll be here at 6 AM. Will that be ok, Madam?"

"Sure." Abha dropped her fingers from the door, and the hinge got the door to close, leaving a hollow sound in the room.

She walked to the bathroom and turned on the geyser to get lukewarm water for a shower. Water poured down, tangling her yet tangled hair as her fingers combed through them, taking a little shampoo from her travel-size shampoo sachet. While taking a shower, within her mind, she started to make a list of important grocery items that she would need to purchase. Her black-inked tattoo looked even darker when she rubbed a layer of moisturizer on her skin. Coming out in her favorite turquoise towel, she looked for a pair of jeans and her black tank top when a sound from a guitar caught her attention. She felt curious, and the sound became prominent with a chorus vocal joining the guitar. She walked toward the kitchen. Her mind felt refreshed, and she tapped her feet to the beat. Her watch left on the kitchen aisle showed 9 PM and made her aware of how late it was since she really ate something wholesome. She broke off the dance and slid into her usual flip-flop that she pulled out from the side zipper of her travel bag. She headed toward the main door with the key to the door jiggling in her hand. Her red cross-body fossil bag and wet hair tied into a messy bun on the top of her head made her look classy.

She thought of chugging down the stairs but feeling her hunger-level she opted for the elevator.

The group of musical boys' attention drew to her when she cheered them with a thumbs up while entering the elevator. They looked at each other, probably feeling lucky by a sudden glimpse of a sexy woman.

On the 6th floor, the lift door opened up, and a man, probably in his twenties, got in. Big eyes, fuller lips and dark eyebrows, tanned complexion, he looked a little perplexed seeing Abha in the elevator. For a moment, he was hesitant to get in and took a step back, but when the door was about to close, Abha pressed the open button again, and he got in. He settled in one corner, lowering his gaze to the floor of the elevator.

When Abha smiled at him, he smiled back, but a kind of timid look still dominated his appearance. The elevator wall had an advertisement for a nearby meat shop from where Abha could order fresh chicken and fish, so she captured an image of it and instantly called the number. Bad signal disturbed her call on and off. She wanted to place an order for half a kilogram of chicken and a kilogram of river fish from them. At the ground floor, when the elevator door opened up, Abha decided to say 'Hello' to the guy.

"Hello, I'm new here. My name is Abha!" she reached out to shake his hand when the guy looked at her in a shy manner. The elevator door closed with a soothing bell sound.

"Akhil! Nice meeting you!" he smiled, and then he took a different exit toward the parking area whereas Abha walked toward the main gate to explore the nearby restaurants.

After a quick carryout from a local dhaba, Abha walked back into the apartment premises and went to the only grocery shop that was inside the society. Since it was around 10 PM at night, the shop was not overly crowded. An elderly, extra nice shopkeeper welcomed her. A couple of masks were displayed at the entrance of the shop from where Abha picked up a black and a beige one. The shopkeeper went on bragging about his shop when she looked around and tried to find the availability of the things that she would need on a regular basis.

"Everything is available here, Madam! Just name it!" he announced proudly when his two young assistants giggled standing at the corner of the shop. With masks on their faces, they all looked so similar that if Abha saw them the next day she would hardly recognize them.

Abha smiled at them, making them a little conscious.

"I would also need two packets of toned milk." She kept the rest of the items on his tiny counter.

"Madan... two packets of toned milk!" He shrilled in a weird voice when Abha's eyes went to the top rack on the cigarette section. Even though she wasn't a full-time smoker, once in a while she gave company to her friends or if she was too bored she would take a puff or two to get rid of her stress. It was one such day, and she stared at the Marlboro lights.

"Madam, see this new mouth freshener. It will melt in your tongue! It's totally new in the market!" The shopkeeper advertised seeing her eyes on that section.

"Sure. So a pack of Marlboro lights and two packs of the new mouth freshener!" Abha yanked open her purse to take the cash out when one of the store boys gaped at her.

"Sorry Madam, I don't have a big bag for you. Here everybody brings their own bags. Please bring one from next time" He opened a paper bag and stuffed in most of the things in that except the cigarette pack and the bread, which he handed her separately.

"Sure! Thank you so much!" Abha clutched the bag and the rest of the things and descended the shop stairs and walked toward the elevator. Few dogs barked, chasing one another while the shopkeeper asked his boys to start wrapping up the vegetables displayed outside the shop since it was close to their closing time.

Abha's phone rang aloud when she was about to get to the elevator.

"Hi Khushi!"

"Hey Abha! How are you finding your new flat? Anyone interesting?" Kushi, Abha's friend, shrilled from the other end.

"Yeah…yeah! What do you think?" Abha chuckled, and the security guard gave her a strange stare.

"Listen babe… I'll get home and call you! So hold your curiosity for a minute!" Abha's yet energetic voice told.

Abha opted to climb up the stairs and hence pulled the rugged door that led her to the stairs. Probably only a few people used the stairs, and hence the door felt pretty jammed and rusted. The stairs were clean but smelled of closed air. She chugged up the stairs, but at the 5th floor, her legs started to feel tired.

Come on, Abha! You can do it!

She tried to motivate herself when a distinct smell of smoke felt strong in her nose. Two teenage boys were sitting on the steps that ran from the fifth to the sixth floor. Seeing Abha, they looked at her, scanning her from bottom to top. One of them elbowed the other, and the other guy was trying to do a flirtatious eye contact with her.

Abha went one step ahead. "Do you have a lighter?" She asked one of them, her eyes had an attitude, and her lips drawn straight.

The second boy handed a matchbox to her. She lit a cigarette and drew a satisfying puff from it, leaving rings of smoke reminiscent in the air.

She handed over the matchbox and walked up the stairs; their eyes and gaping mouths trailed her until she vanished from their sight.

Five more floors, and then she reached her door.

She stubbed out the cigarette at the disposer next to the elevator and fished out the keys to the door. The cigarette smell took over the corridor air suddenly.

Popping in a mouth freshener, when she creaked open the door, a small shadow stood right behind her. She jittered in fear.

Shit! The word escaped her lips without her knowledge. She turned around and saw a tiny, hardly six years old girl standing there, grinning broadly at her.

"Are you the new tenant?" she walked up to Abha, and her cheeks gleamed under the corridor light. Her half-broken front teeth looked very cute on her.

"Yes! What is your name?" Abha shook hands with the adorable child when a strange shriek, as if someone was calling out a name, wafted through her ears.

"Tina… Tina…"

A woman in her thirties, wearing a saree, hair neatly combed and swirled into a bun at the nape of her neck, came out hurriedly. Her bright purple synthetic saree with the tight drape and the edge of the saree tucked up at one side of her slender hip and a big dark orange bindi, a serving spoon in hand, gave her a homely look. Her voice sounded tensed, but as soon as she saw her daughter, it instantly changed into a strict motherly tone. When she turned further to her right and saw Abha, she felt perplexed for a second before flaunting a conscious smile.

She untucked the edge of the saree and covered her already covered sleeves and pulled her daughter into her arms. "Hello ji!" A bouncy musical greeting smoothed Abha's ears.

"Hello… Nice to meet your daughter! She is very adorable!" Abha brushed her delicate fingers on the girl's soft cheeks with affection. And then she cursed herself, thinking she shouldn't have touched her during those awful COVID days. But the mother seemed to be cool with it.

"Aunty ko apna naam batao!" she patted her daughter's shoulder.

"Arpita Nagar!"

"Nice to meet you, Arpita!" Abha smiled at both daughter and mother. "Your frock is very cute…" Arpita ran her fingers through the shiny sequined frills of her own frock and gave them a proud stare. The ladies got involved in comfortable small talks, as a man in white cotton trousers and a pale yellow shirt showed up almost suddenly, leaving a strong pungent smell from the paan (betel).

"Who are you talking to?" The middle-aged man, seemingly in his forties, asked. He had curious big eyes. A paleness overshadowed the mother and daughter's smile instantly, which Abha didn't fail to notice. They took a few steps back from Abha, settling at the corner of the door. It looked to her as if they were trying to leave a way to some VIP.

"I'm Dilip Nagar! And you?" his hands folded across his chest, and hence Abha didn't reach out to offer a shake hand.

"Abha, new tenant here." She smiled as the man eyed the lady to go inside the house with her daughter, which worked just like magic, and they scurried back in without wasting a second. Arpita waved at Abha on the way back, but her mom eyed her immediately.

His obvious stare, especially when he scanned her tattoo, sleeveless tank top, and the pack of Marlboro, felt strange to her.

"With family?" his second question shot her, almost meeting her expectations.

"No, alone!" She said with a straight face. She opened the door balancing her stuff in one hand. His brief and cold reaction were not shocking to her, but she felt sad for the lady and the child.

Gosh!

She dumped all the things on the dining table and took a big bite from the chicken roll and leaned onto the blue sofa. She clubbed two sofa cushions and shoved them behind her neck and laid down in a relaxed position when a quarreling voice drifted in the air, catching her attention, and she walked to the balcony following the sound.

"This is the reason I wanted a boy! Look at the girls these days! Skin showing… tattoo… smoke… what not! I don't want Tina to go to her flat, and you too are definitely staying away from that witch!

"Bloody moron!" An instant anger raged through Abha's blood as she felt like dodging the balcony and shattering that man's bald head.

Loser!

Her inner voice echoed within her mind.

She finished the roll within a minute and walked to the kitchen basin to fetch some water from the purifier when, once again, her phone rang out loud in the empty house.

"Hey Khushi!" she smiled, but still, that neighbor's voice created some nasty ripples in her mind.

Two friends spoke for hours as Abha mentioned the good and bad encounters that she experienced during her first day of her stay at the new apartment. When she hung up the call, her boyfriend Animesh called her, but she was too tired by then and needed a lie-in badly.

She drifted off to sleep while her subconscious mind kept thinking about all the characters she came across.

Chapter 2

The doorbell rang annoyingly for the fourth time and woke her up. Abha sprang up from the crumpled bedsheet and rushed to the door. The weather of Delhi started to get a little chilly, and she craved for her favorite quilt, which looked to be missing.

It must have gone missing at the time of packing and shifting, thoughts rumbled in her mind.

Rubbing her sleepy eyes, when she opened the door, her new maid Susheela was standing at her doorstep with a curious face. The yellow of her bright red saree matched well with her yellow blouse, and she looked like a sunflower in Abha's eyes for a moment.

"Were you sleeping? I thought you wouldn't open the door!" She said with a grin, walking straight to the kitchen. The rhythmic sound of her ankle trailed her footsteps. Abha left the door ajar, and the hinge closed it automatically. She followed her to the kitchen.

"Is there someone else in your house?" Susheela asked curiously when she saw the door to the second bedroom closed.

Abha furrowed her brows and avoided replying to the intriguing question. "Please give me some coffee and wash the utensils." Susheela's happy face, seeing only one set of plate and mug in the sink, was obvious. Abha went to the sofa with her phone, browsing through her social media accounts. Susheela started to broom the balcony after keeping the milk on the stove for boiling.

When Abha finally walked to the washbasin and splashed cold water on her face to get rid of the sleepiness, a loud chanting from her neighbor's house startled her.

"Dilip Sir, very religious and never forgets to do his morning rituals!" Susheela eyed with pride, pointing next door when a burning smell from the kitchen caught their attention.

"Oh God! Milk!" They rushed to the kitchen, and Abha turned off the half-burned milk.

"Come on! Why are you doing other works leaving the milk on the oven?" Abha gushed at Susheela when Priya, her cook, walked in wearing a yellow salwar.

"Oh Dear! Yellow again!" Abha's conscious echoed.

Both the maids started to bicker with each other on the milk topic when Abha made her way to the closed boxes, which still held her belongings, showpieces, crystals, and utensils. She decided to ignore them and hence shoved in her Bluetooth earplugs, listening to Ed Sheeran's latest numbers.

"Is the coffee done?" she asked for the second time when Priya hurried up from the kitchen with a mug full of coffee and some biscuits in a small bowl.

Hearing the clink of her favorite chime, Susheela peeped in from the balcony.

"Abha madam, let me call the maintenance office. They will come and fix all these for you! You might need a couple of nails on the walls for hanging the showpieces." She voluntarily walked to the intercom for dialing the number to the apartment maintenance office without even looking for Abha's response. Susheela's point made sense to Abha, even though her approach was beyond her understanding. Abha dropped the chime back into the box and took a sip from her moderately hot coffee and switched on the Television. She shuffled through a few channels in a preoccupied mind when a knock on the door made her conscious. She pulled on a shrug around her slim body. Carpenter, Arvind, came in with his toolbox, and Susheela flashed a smirk which he ignored.

"Madam, my name is Arvind. I do all kinds of utility works in this society." Arvind removed his slippers and dropped his toolbox at a corner next to the door and took a quick peek at the interior.

"I have a couple of chimes and a wall clock that you need to fix." Abha maneuvered through the boxes to open the first box from the door. Arvind nodded, but his blank expressions gave Abha a hint that he was not very familiar with the word *"Chimes."*

Susheela did her share of talking, explaining him more about chimes, making him feel further embarrassed. His big eyes had some kind of rawness to them, and a mask covered his face. Abha wondered how he would look if the mask wasn't there on his face.

They located a few suitable spots on the wall for the clock, chimes, and the rest of the wall hangings when a teenage boy, of age somewhere between 16 to 20, walked across the corridor for the second time. He looked at Abha through the ajar door with a smile on his face.

"Can I help you?" Abha walked up to the door.

"Ma'am, do you want to get any dusting work done?" he asked politely with a naïve voice.

"Umm... not right now. But let me know your number so that I can call you if I need to get some done." Abha fished out her phone from the back pocket of her denim shorts. The boy took a quick peek at her slender legs.

"Tell me your number." Abha punched the number. The boy stuttered a couple of times while telling his own number. The small girl from the next house smiled at Abha from their door, and Abha waved at her, but a rush of footsteps came out prominent, and Abha looked over her shoulder. It was Susheela.

"Madam, I'll do the dusting if needed. Please don't give any work to anyone else." She demanded. With a mopping stick in hand and with unkempt hair that looked like a lion's mane, she almost picked up a fight with the teenage boy, and in that process of stopping her maid, she mistakenly dialed the number she had just saved. The small kid, probably scared of the bicker, scurried back to the corridor. His phone rang aloud from Abha's call.

Abha slammed the door in anger and gave an ultimatum to Susheela for unnecessarily involving herself in everything. The day already looked to have started on a hectic note. Susheela quietly walked back to her work, and Arvind took his leave after fixing the clock and chimes. The clock went on the wall above the dining table, and the rest of the hall and chimes were hung on some suitable places too. The soothing jingle from the chimes made Abha happy when she asked for another cup of coffee from her cook Priya.

Her cellphone vibrated.

"Hey Animesh! Sorry, I dozed off… couldn't pick your call." Abha walked to her bedroom picking up her phone while drumming up an explanation on why she couldn't talk to Animesh the previous night. Closing the door on her way to the bedroom for getting some privacy while talking to her boyfriend made the maids curious. Susheela eyed Priya as the bedroom door closed.

"Boyfriend!" Priya grinned.

"So, *the new girl in the city!* How do you feel there?" His heavy voice drawled, curving up a smile on Abha's face.

"So far so good! So when are you planning to visit?" She lied down, stretching her body with a sensual moan. Her fingers went to the curls of her hair.

"Wish now! Are you inviting me?" a subdued smile came from his side and made her blush.

"Why not, Mr. Saluja! You're most welcome!" Abha smiled cheekily, got to her feet, and walked toward the closet to find a dress to wear to the office.

"I was thinking if we could meet on weekends…" A frail knock on the bedroom door broke their conversation.

When she opened the door, she saw Arvind standing there.

Abha, feeling a bit strange, thinking why Susheela or Priya didn't talk to him before letting him knock her bedroom door.

"What is it?" Abha Asked with a straight face. "Who's that?" Animesh's voice came from the other side.

"I'll call you back!" Abha dropped the call and grabbed her stole. She wrapped it around her semitransparent top when Arvind gazed down, feeling a bit embarrassed.

"Madam, your clock doesn't have a battery. I happened to have a few with me, so thought of checking with you if you needed one." he said politely, still looking down.

"Oh! I'm so sorry! Yes, I do need some batteries for it. Thanks, Arvind!" She said with an apologetic voice when Susheela walked in from the balcony located behind the kitchen.

"What happened?" her usual query started.

Abha ignored it, and so did Arvind. He took a stool and carefully unfolded a newspaper on it before climbing on the same for reaching the clock level.

Chapter 3

First day at her new Office:

"Come on in!" Phillip's confident drawl filled the air when Abha knocked his chamber's door. Abha's colleague cum new friend Nupur looked at her with raised eyebrows as she handed over a bunch of printouts.The coffee vending machine adjacent to Abha's boss Phillip Alexander's cabin was like a hotspot for the ladies in the office. Nupur was actively keeping an eye on Philip and seeking his attention, as were the other women in the office.

"Hey Phillip!"

He's so hot! Abha's internal voice echoed when she saw Phillip in person. Husky voice, long beard, and a salt and pepper ponytail with a stark face and gray eyes, he could be a taller and smarter replacement for many of the huge meathead heroes these days. Abha spoke to Phillip multiple times over the phone but never got a chance to meet him in person.

"Welcome to Delhi! Hope you are finding it comfortable here!" His fuller grip held her palm with warmth.

"A pretty cool place indeed!" Abha kept her leather backpack on the chair beside her and sat across his new boss, Phillip.

"So all settled? Can we talk about our new project then?" He asked with a hint of a Russian accent. His Russian mom's and Konkani father's love affair became viral when he initially joined that company.

"Sure, it's my first solo project on photography. I'd love to discuss the plan and take guidance from your experience! Also, I have done some homework on the same and would like to show you before we begin the discussion!" Abha handed him the printouts gracefully.

"Impressive!" His raised eyebrows. His welcoming smile felt comforting to Abha.

"Thanks!" Her eyes shone bright with energy. She looked around admiring the interior of his office. The antique decors with a combo of wood and metal works on the walls set a trendy yet classy taste for her boss.

"A Pictorial project on the tribals in Assam! Your assignment looks great! Why don't you talk to Azhar? He will be able to assist you during the whole trip!" Phillip's gaze raised to Abha while she was still admiring his room.

"Looks like you like my office more than me!" Phillip's mild chuckle with a witty sense of humor embarrassed her for a second.

"I must say you have a great taste in interior design... beautiful office!" Abha smiled, and Phillip nodded with a humble gesture. "I'll talk to Azhar on the same and probably fix up a trip for him and me sometime next week to Shillong." Abha's confidence impressed Phillip.

"There you go, Girl!" Phillip pushed some more papers across the table along with the old ones.

"Thanks, Phillip!" She smiled and got to her feet preparing to leave his chamber.

"Hey Abha! How about a quick coffee at 5?" Phillip's abrupt offer of sharing his coffee time felt a little strange to her. He was rumored to be a bit on the choosy side.

"Why not?" Abha's heart skipped a beat. "But maybe tomorrow if you are available! You know, I was thinking of setting a meeting with Azar today itself for discussing on the project." She wanted to take it slow. Her kohl-rimmed eyes replied with confidence.

"Sure, tomorrow it is then!" Phillip's witty smile lingered in Abha's mind for the rest of the day.

"So how's your meeting with Phillip?" Nupur asked while they both settled in the cafeteria during a mid-day break.

"He's gorgeous!" Abha said, her slender fingers ran through her sleek arm. For once she thought about how it would be to date her boss.

"I told you!" Nupur exuded excitement in her voice but Abha's lost look bothered her.

"What happened, lost Island?" She gave Abha's arm a quick jerk sipping her cold coffee. Her turtleneck pink sweater looked a little heavy for the mild winter.

"Umm… I think he was asking me out on a coffee date?" Abha's half-cheek blush caught her friend's eyeballs.

"What? He just asked you out?" Nupur's overexcited reaction was so obvious that Abha cursed herself the next moment for sharing the coffee date matter.

"Come on! Not asked me out or anything like that. He was just asking if I could join him for a coffee because he wanted to discuss something on the upcoming project." Abha's eyes were still glued on Nupur's overly excited expression.

"Interesting enough! He never asked anyone else in the office to have coffee with him to discuss stuff!" Nupur's deliberately shocked expression gave Abha a further blush. "Hey, gotta leave… so much work to be sorted!" She walked to the trash to toss her paper cup.

"Of course!" Nupur winked with a crisp smirk at Abha.

"Come on!" The banters kept going as they both walked to their desks.

After a long day at the office when Abha walked up ten floors in the confines of her apartment building, a tranquil ambience and the same musty smell oozed from the rarely used corridor. But it all started to feel familiar to her already.

On the way, she bumped into her new neighbor, the little girl, Tina, and her mother, who still was a little hesitant to talk to her. Abha smiled and brushed her fingers through the little girl's silky hair before unlocking the front door. Tina waved at her, and then they slowly vanished from her sight. Abha opened the door, dropped her bag, and walked up to the kitchen for a strong coffee.

The park opposite to her society building tempted her for a brisk walk, and hence Abha got ready, sliding into her black sports bra and matching shorts with a pink crop top. Shoving the earplugs of the microphones when she walked in the park, the men in and around the park felt motivated instantly.

For the first round, she went for a brisk walk, and then when she started her second round with a jog, a pair of eyes caught her attention. He was a middle-aged man. He was walking in the park clutching a bunch of papers in his hand. His eyes met Abha's eyes each time they crossed each other's ways in the oval-shaped walkway. A blue mask was covering his nose and mouth. But his eyes were enlightened, and it seemed to her as if he was intending to crack a conversation with Abha.

After three rounds of jogging, when Abha rested on a bench to do her usual breathing exercises, a hand touched her shoulder, startling her. It was getting duskier, and not many people were present in the park.

She looked over her shoulder and found the same middle-aged man standing right behind her.

"Yes!" she said, getting up from the green bench. Her eyes making a confident contact with his eyes.

"Hello, my name is Ranjan Ghosh, and I stay here..." His finger pointed toward the next building where Abha lived.

"Sure. Hello." She reached to shake his hand.

"Are you new to this place?" Followed his second question.

"Umm... yes." Abha said hesitating a bit to reveal the truth that she was new to this area.

When Abha ushered him to sit, he took his seat on the same bench. She moved a couple of inches when Mr. Ghosh sat next to her to give him more room. His spiritual talk and holistic interest gave her a positive vibe. After a couple of minutes of talking, when he handed her a sheet,

Abha unfolded it to open. It showed information about an event.

"5k running event! Run for a cause!" He announced. His heavy voice sounded poised, steady yet calm. His eye contact was strong and sincere.

"Are you joining the event too?" Asked Abha.

"Wish I could!" He gazed down. "I am a patient of Parkinson! And Going to these kinds of events is a whole day affair! So I generally don't join, but I do encourage youngsters like you who still have the ability to change the world or do at least their part to the change!" he went on, and Abha kept listening to his calm voice. "By the way, for you, this should be just a piece of cake! I just saw you running, and I must say that you are a good runner… good energy and nice stamina!" His speech instantly gave her a proud feeling.

Abha smiled with a nod. "Thank you, Mr. Ghosh! I will try my best to join the event unless anything urgent comes up." She leaped up to her feet, batting away some mosquitoes that made their way around her legs.

"Sure! And thank you!" He acknowledged and turned around toward the other gate of the park. Abha felt quite inspired and spiritual after meeting that enlightened soul, Mr. Ghosh.

Back at home, when Animesh called and Abha told him about Phillip and Mr. Ghosh. He wasn't feeling very happy about her whole decision to move to Delhi. But he refrained himself from conveying that to Abha. He knew that Abha was an independent girl and hence he wanted to give her the space to grow independently.

"So what else did your Mr. Ghosh say apart from the running event? By the way, you must participate. 5K run is like a piece of cake for you! Isn't it?"

"You know, Mr. Ghosh said the same thing!" Abha's repeated mention about Mr. Ghosh agitated him.

"Good for you!" Animesh's possessive mind echoed in her ear. "You don't love me anymore!" He said after a short silence, which got Abha back to their usual daily bicker.

"Come on, Animesh! We had enough discussions on that! You know I love you, and I'm not running away from you for Christ's sake! Please try and understand!" Abha walked to the fridge to fetch a bottle of coke, her voice edgy.

"I was just kidding! Hey…"

"I'm listening!"

"I miss you! When are you coming to Mumbai?" Animesh's voice came from the other end.

"Very soon!" She sighed.

"How about making it virtually until then?" his voice almost whispered.

"Come on Ani! You are sounding desperate now!" Abha turned on the geyser switch and leaned, holding the bathroom door frame to check if the geyser light turned green or not.

"I am! I am missing our old times…" His voice was seductive.

"Umm… I'm gonna have a shower and be right back! Why don't you get ready by then? Let's catch up!" Abha took a bite from the nutty chocolate bar. Animesh smirked from the other end. She stopped in front of the huge round mirror in her living room. Curls of her messy hair went about her face, and her face appeared glossy from the sunscreen lotion; she looked absolutely gorgeous. She blushed to her own self.

"Can I see you in 15 minutes?"

"Sure." Abha made her way to the shower, dropping her top on the way into the hamper. Her body and mind were ready for an intimacy.

Chapter 4

Months later:

Tr....ring!

The landline phone rang out loud when Susheela strode straight out of the bathroom with soaked hands. She left the tap on, which made a constant annoying dripping noise.

"Hello..." her rural accent added an edgy hint to the greeting.

Abha, snuggled in the layers of quilt, sat on the sofa and sipped from the health drink that her cook just handed her a couple of minutes ago. Mild fever associated with a bad cold irked her as she took the soft cloth to blow her nose.

"Yes, talk to madam!" Susheela handed over the phone to Abha and walked back to the bathroom to continue with her cleaning work.

"Yes. May I know who's talking?" Abha's broken voice, down with cold and sore throat, struggled to speak.

"This is regarding the online appointment that you have booked with Dr. Karthik Sudhaker. The doctor will be available this afternoon at 3 pm. Can I confirm the appointment ma'am?" A polite voice drifted from the other side.

"Sure! I'll be there at 3." Considering the Covid factor, she didn't want to delay seeing a doctor. Abha hung up and went back to her blanket and the TV remote. Her mind felt like listening to some old Hindi songs.

A howling gale took the shape of a cyclone when Susheela ran to close the balcony doors. A few pigeons fluttered their wings, finding it difficult to sit on the window shield due to the extreme weather. The TV signal went on and off, and finally, the power gave in.

Abha stretched her limbs before getting to her feet and prepared to take a quick shower before going to the hospital. A bad headache chafed her forehead, but ignoring that, she got ready to go out.

"Shall I come with you?" Susheela asked with concern.

"No, Susheela! I should be just ok! You can go home. Did Priya finish her work too?" Abha applied a mild shade of her Estee Lauder lipstick and gave her lips a quick rub.

"She's done too. We are planning to go together, so that was we can share the umbrella. You take care ma'am and please call me if you need anything." Susheela walked to the door after collecting trash. Priya was still filling drinking water from the water purifier. As they both left, the door closed with a hollow sound, leaving an emptiness in the whole flat.

Abha opted to take the elevator instead of stairs. The security guard opened the car door as she slid into the backseat of the Uber that drove her to the nearby hospital. A splash of rain dampened her curly hair, and she walked into the hospital corridor to see Dr. Karthik Sudhakar.

"May I come in?" asked Abha, taking a peek into the doctor's office. A nurse stood next to her, ushering her to get in. "This way," she seemed to be in a hurry.

"Please come in! Take your seat." He pushed the small steel stool toward Abha with a courteous smile. "So, what brings you here?" He pulled his chair closer. His features were sharp, with thick eyebrows, sharp eyes, and prim lips with dusky complexion gave an indication of sheer intelligence. His fingers lingered a little longer when checking her vitals, his talk a bit flirtatious which made Abha blush a couple of times during their conversations. He had a unique smile which looked interesting to her.

"Looks to be a viral. The germs are hovering in the air during the rainy seasons. I don't think any Covid test is required at this moment but just keep an eye if the symptoms persist longer than three days. "You can just continue with your usual routine. I'll write a simple medication, and you can collect it from the front desk." He removed his latex gloves and washed his hands when Abha admired his toned structure.

"Thanks, doc! Umm… actually, there was another thing that I wanted to talk about." Abha bit her lips, thinking whether to talk about the problem.

"Sure. Tell me! Not a boyfriend problem right?" He winked, which made her laugh out loud.

"No… I have Attention Deficit Disorder, and I would like to see a doctor for that. Also, I find it hard to fall asleep…" Abha half-ended her statement, giving a mild smile on his face.

"Let's do blood tests and also a Toad test for ruling out sleep apnea." He shoved another piece of paper in her folder after writing the test orders.

"Try doing some deep breathing before hitting the bed. No hectic exercises before sleeping!" With a witty smile, he handed over a small sample bottle of sanitizer and a couple of medications from his medicine cabinet that seemed to store more than hundreds of medications.

"Are you a good sleeper?" Abha asked with a smile. It just came out spontaneously.

"Ha ha ha... see you in a week then!" He avoided replying to her query. Abha made her way out when his eyes trailed her. She looked over her shoulder to spare him a glance. He smiled, and so did she. There was something strange about his eyes, Abha thought to herself.

As she came out of the main door of the clinic, her phone beeped out with a vibration. An auto pulled over to pick her up when Abha fished out her phone to read the message.

"How are you, gorgeous? What are you doing in the hospital?" The message read. She instantly looked around to locate anyone suspicious.

Everything appeared to be normal. Late afternoon time and vehicles rushed mercilessly, increasing both noise and air pollution.

"Who's this?" She replied while entering the auto-rickshaw. The driver looked at the sky and murmured something within his mind.

No reply came after her message. After about ten minutes of drive, she reached her apartment building. The rain looked to take a break, but it was still drizzling. After crossing the main entrance on the way to her elevator, when her umbrella failed to work, Abha planned to run to the elevator while a series of thudding footfalls became prominent to her ears. She looked around, and it was Akhil, the young man whom she met in the elevator on the first day of her stay.

"Hey... wait!" He sounded more confident than last time. Extending the umbrella, he gestured Abha to get inside the same. Abha wondered if he had enrolled in a crush course on confidence.

"How have you been? It's been a long time!" Abha smiled, walking under his umbrella. Her teary eyes from fever drew attention and sympathy from Akhil.

"Is everything ok? Aren't you well?" He asked curiously.

"Yes. Just a mild fever." Abha smiled; her kohl started to smudge beyond the rim of her eyes, boosting her sensuality.

"I thought you were a very reserved person!" Abha added. Her curiosity raised seeing his radical change in behavior.

"I got a new job!" Akhil said, smiling.

"I see! That's great news! Congratulations!" Abha shook hands with him. The dampness of her fingers stayed in his warm hand for some time.

A quiet walk to the elevator under the same umbrella and the confines of the elevator made them a little uncomfortable.

"So where's my treat?" She asked, trying to crack another conversation.

"Anytime. Whenever you want." He smiled. His eyes checking out Abha's damp hair, trailing her wide hazel eyes, gazing at her slender hips, and then to her high heels.

"Are you twins?" Abha asked, seeing the drastic change in his behavior.

He laughed out!

"Thanks for sharing your umbrella and please come over sometime!" Abha waved at him while getting off the elevator, and Akhil reciprocating the same. A hint of warmth dominated his smile.

Her languid body stretched again, settling down on the couch when another message flashed on her phone.

"Why visiting Doctor? Are you pregnant?" The sudden strange messages from the unknown number freaked her out. A gush of anger ran down her spine all of a sudden.

What the fuck!

"Who the hell are you?" She typed in so fast, jumbling up a couple of words here and there.

"You are gorgeous! I admire you…" Abha threw her phone on the sofa and went around her house visiting each room, checking the locks of each and every door and window. Nothing looked unusual. She planned not to reply to those idiotic messages.

That looked to be the last creepy message from that unknown number, and Abha thought it was over.

But a few weeks later:

Knock… knock!

Somebody was at her door when Abha was relaxing on her balcony with a book in hand. Her eyelids went heavy after reading a couple of pages. She wanted to sleep away the Sunday afternoon, but an interesting plot from the book kept her awake, still feeling lazy.

She was supposed to meet her boss Phillip over dinner that evening which just got canceled and postponed to the next day. She dropped the book on the side table. Her mind was virtually browsing through her closet to find decent evening wear when the tapping sound on the door became prominent to her ears.

"Coming!" She responded, walking toward the door. The pink shorts and white tank top with a pink and white striped shirt on top of the white top exposed a fair amount of her skin. Sleeves folded up to the elbow and a messy bun at the top of her head gave her a gorgeous yet casual look. Her high hip bones and little exposed skin between the top and the shorts were capable of capturing a thousand eyes.

"Coming…." She repeated and yanked open the door, finding Akhil standing right there with a box in his hand.

"Hey… what's up?" She said, surprised to see him at her doorstep.

"Hey… I just thought of stopping by…" He stammered a little bit when Abha flashed a gorgeous smile, ushering him into the living room.

He rested the small box on the dining table and looked around when Abha closed the door. Her neighbor Mr. Nagar gaped at her with shock when he saw Akhil entering her flat. He almost stood frozen there for a couple of minutes when Abha slammed the door to close.

"Beautiful interior!" Akhil looked around. "Thank you!" Abha smiled and asked him to sit on the couch and walked to the kitchen to get a glass of water for him. "Feel free to watch TV." She handed the remote before walking to the kitchen.

Priya had just finished her regular chores and walked out after packing and shoving the previous night's leftover food into her jute bag. She walked her way to the elevator. Her neighbor, who was still standing there with a curious face, felt embarrassed after seeing Priya and scurried back into his house.

"So what's the occasion? I can smell cake in that box!" Abha's pitch, a little loud, came from the kitchen when Akhil tried to figure out how to navigate to the guide section on her TV remote.

"It's my treat for finally bagging a job! I wasn't very sure if you would like a whole cake, so I just got a piece for you," said Akhil.

"Sweet! Btw, it depends on what flavored cake that is. If it's a triple-layer chocolate fudge, I can finish the whole thing in one sitting, but definitely not the other ones." Abha came back with a glass of water for Akhil and a bottle of wine and two glasses balancing in both her hands.

"Drinks?" Abha offered, and Akhil nodded with a smile. "Sure."

Abha poured the wine precisely into the crystal glasses and opened a packet of spicy potato chips and a few slices of cheese that she bought from a fancy nut shop the last time she went to the Habitat center.

Akhil tuned on a music channel when Abha walked to the balcony to light a smoke. Akhil followed.

"The view from your flat is beautiful!" Akhil leaned over the railing. He looked at her smoke, and she handed him the same smartly controlling her snigger that made its way to her lips seeing the amateur way of holding the cigarette. A drag from it gave him a sudden awkward cough.

"Hey, you ok?" Abha rushed to the kitchen and got him another glass of water and rubbed his back when Akhil felt a bit embarrassed.

"You shouldn't have smoked!" She giggled. Their small talk continued for about an hour.

The wine kind of took over as they got comfortable with each other. A dusky chilly weather felt perfect for a smoke and wine. Akhil leaned on Abha's shoulder. Smiles brushed through both their lips. He took another puff from her cigarette. This time it was nice and smooth. His eyes looked drowsy from the wine.

"See, it's not rocket science!" He took the cigarette and placed it on the ashtray that was kept in one corner of the balcony.

Abha's phone rang, and she took a peek to check the number on her phone.

Animesh!

Abha murmured when Akhil took Abha's hand and suddenly drew her close. Her phone fell on the chair.

"Hey! Easy boy!" Abha's face came closer to his face, her eyes looking into Akhil's.

"You know, you are the first girl I'm having a drink with!" Akhil whispered, pulling her even closer, feeling the scent of breath.

"I can see that!" She smiled, tried to pull away gently, but his grip was surprisingly firm.

A void air went silent for a couple of seconds, raising their heartbeats. The back of Abha's throat throttled hearing her phone ring again.

"This is beautiful!" His grip went firmer.

Abha stared at him. She was double-minded whether to encourage him or not.

Akhil's lips skimmed along her neck, traveling to the shoulder, pushing the unbuttoned shirt off her shoulder.

"You really want to do this?" Abha tried to fight her gush of hormones.

"I don't know!" But his gaze darkened on her.

The usual chorus voice of kids from their neighbor's flat drifted in the air and made them smile.

"Let's go inside!" Abha said. Her fingers interlaced his, pulling him to the sofa. Abha liked the feeling of whatever was happening, and they both landed next to each other, flumping down on the couch. Her fingers tugged the balcony door, pulling it closed, and then took a last sip from her wine.

Akhil took another sip. Their eyes locked as if they are inviting each other for a deep intimacy. A strange chill ran down Abha's spine, and she felt that she had been craving for sex since some time then.

Akhil's lips kissed her lips with passion. She moaned. His fingers combed through her tangled curls in a tight grip. Abha's breathing pitched high, enjoying the closeness, exploring the taste of his wine-sipped mouth. Their bodies layered each other with wild passion. The tug of his fingers pulled her shirt off and made the way to her bare skin. The touch of his tongue on her flat stomach clenched her muscles, and a soothing moan escaped her mouth.

Abha moaned in pleasure over and over. As his fingers traveled down on her, exploring the heat of her body, she clutched his hair pulling him closer, feeling his breath on her skin. Abha enjoyed every bit of the romance. Her hands tried to push his trousers down, when Akhil loosened the belt, assisting her.

A deep romance took over and followed an erotic lovemaking, plunging into the depth of the couch under the dim light of the hall.

The both were exhausted after the prolonged session of love.

"I think it went too fast! I've just met you twice!" she said sliding back into her shirt.

Akhil got up, buttoning up his linen trousers, thoughtful.

"You should go now! I need to think about it!" Abha held the door open, which came like a sudden shock to Akhil.

"Please taste the cake! And I am sorry if I've troubled you." He walked out slowly after grabbing his socks and shoes. The door hinge closed with an annoying sound.

Abha sat on the sofa, furrowing her eyebrows, thinking why the heck she was so desperate. Why she couldn't control her urge. The night darkened further, and more mosquitoes started coming in when she got up and closed the windows.

Chapter 5

"Great job! Keep it up Ms. Shanyal!" Her boss, Phillip, patted her back, smiling. Abha acknowledged with a nod. "Btw, your next project would be exploring a village in the southern side, so gear up, Lady! It cheered up Abha, and her boss strode back to his chamber.

"Hey Phillip! These are a few new images!" Abha turned around, springing up to her feet, but by that time Phillip had vanished from her sight, walking back into his office.

Abha primed up her lips and sat down, plopping back into her chair. Her coffee mug seemed empty, and she exhaled a sigh. A dull squeaking sound from the chair felt very rhythmic to her.

But her phone rang.

"Coffee at 5?" Phillip's husky voice shot from the other side and gave her an embarrassed smile. "What?" She wondered how Philip sensed her obsession for coffee. She looked around to check his presence but couldn't find any. She looked at his office, but nothing, his window blinds were closed.

"Sure!" She replied looking at Nupur who shared her desk and mostly seemed more interested in Phillip's call than her own project deadlines. "What's happening?" She mouthed and Abha eyeballed her, drawing a quick breath.

"And great work, congratulations!" he hung up, leaving Abha a little confused about his 5 PM coffee thing.

"See, he told you… it's a piece of cake for you! You have proved yourself, Girl! And now he's your date! The Greek God Phillip!" Nupur jumped up, her eyes still on Abha.

"Come on, Nupur!" Abha smirked at her comment, but her eyes went to her phone that flashed a message icon.

"Wanna see something?" a new message from the same unknown number read.

"Who the hell are you?" She replied angrily, seeing the message from the same unknown number. The messages had been disturbing her for a couple of weeks then.

No reply came. These messages started to bother her on and off, but she wasn't sure what to do about that.

The day got over, and her boss, Phillip, dropped her home after a coffee date at a high-end coffee shop in South Delhi. When they stopped at the traffic signal, again a message made its way to her phone. She didn't bother to see that. Phillip dropped her off at her residence and gave her a warm hug which lingered more than a usual hug and confused Abha a little more. "See you tomorrow!" she smiled and waved at him as he reversed his luxury car. When she walked out of the elevator, one more beep startled her. She ignored it and started looking for the key to her apartment. Her eyes went to the strange person who was standing right in front of her neighbor Mr. Nagar's house. The person had a long beard, neatly combed, which was giving an evident indication of a fake beard, and his neatly worn orange and white dhoti and shawl that almost smelled of aftershave felt not coordinating with his attire. He looked to be some kind of fraud claiming to have deep religious knowledge or a saint. He checked Abha out from the corner of her eyes while the white highlight on his hair felt obvious to her. Mr. Nagar hardly paid any attention to Abha and looked desperate to satisfy that fake saint.

"Babaji, as you said, I have made all the arrangements for the Putraprapti puja." His folded hands showed his eternal respect for the saint as he ushered him into his house.

Putraprapti! Not again!

Abha's inner voice cursed him.

"If puja's done successfully, no one can stop you from having a boy child!" the saint's heavy voice drawled, and his hand raised to bless him as Abha narrowed her eyes in disgust. Her door lock took more than usual to open.

Morons!

The saint kept chanting something while entering his house. His body was toned, his body hair was black with no hint of gray hair anywhere except a few little patches on his head. The door got closed, and Abha too entered home after an exasperated breath and feeling sick about her neighbor.

Abha dropped her bag at the corner of the sofa and made her way to the bathroom to wash her face. Her stomach churned from hunger and the strange belief of her neighbor kept flitting about her brain.

She splashed cold water on her face and looked in the mirror checking her little overgrown eyebrows which needed a trim. She changed into black shorts and a lilac top and buttoned up her usual striped shirt on top. Tying a messy bun and posing a cigarette between her fingers, she sat on a lounge chair in the balcony and craved for another strong coffee. Both Susheela and Priya had taken off due to Guru Poornima, and hence she had to power through the evening all alone.

Her eyes read a few lines from the mystery novel she got from Khushi during their last meeting. Suddenly a high-pitched snarl came out loud from the next flat. She kept the book and looked around, but everything went quiet after that short shriek.

Abha went back to her book, but a few random sounds that trailed out of her neighbor's house seeped through her ears, disturbing her concentration. She got to her feet, walked close to the railing toward their side, and tried to take a peek. But she could hardly see anything other than their washed clothes that were hung on the balcony robe for drying.

Nothing looked suspicious to her. But soon after that, a series of knocking sounds became prominent. Her conscience said as if someone there needed help.

"Hello!" Abha said loudly. But no answer came.

Again silence hovered. Everything went quiet.

She walked around fiercely, trying to heed the odd sound that came from Mr. Nagar's flat.

Another scream, and Abha could feel something off about the whole thing.

"Help! Please!" someone screamed again, some female voice came followed by a huge thudding noise.

She quickly walked to her front door and opened it to check if their door was open or not, but all she found there was a pair of old-fashioned traditional slippers. Even though the fashion was old, the slippers looked to be new.

She knocked at the door, but no one came to attend her. She layered her ear on their door, but all she could hear was the monotonous sound from a fan or maybe from a refrigerator. The other two flats were shut with shiny locks hanging from outside. She hardly knew anybody in that whole building. She knew Akhil, but he lived in a different wing.

She rushed back home and went all the way to the balcony again. Another thudding noise followed by a low moan updrafted from Mr. Nagar's house.

Abha grabbed her phone to call the police, but an incoming MMS caught her attention and blew her senses.

Someone had made a video of her and Akhil's intimate incident.

Fuck! A sex video! How could you do that, Akhil?

Instantly in her mind, Akhil came up as the criminal.

Abha crashed down on the chair. Her eyes felt blurred from the shock. Another sound escaped from her neighbor's flat, as if someone got trashed against the door that led to their balcony.

A bad migraine hammered her head. She felt a rush of extreme anger on Akhil after watching the video.

Does that mean the unknown number belonged to Akhil?

Another cry shot out prominent from the next flat, and she planned to dodge the balcony and help that family. She kept aside the MMS thing considering the urgency for help.

Her balcony was separated from theirs' only by a foot and a half. It was not an impossible distance or a task to cross that since Abha was tall, and her well-built body and a confident mind were determined to do so.

Due to panic, she forgot about the option of calling their apartment helpdesk. She prayed to God and scrambled past her balcony, taking a little help from the railing and the sewer pipe. After trying for a couple of minutes, she was at their balcony. Her heart thumped, but her mind was still occupied thinking about the video.

How could you do that, Akhil? You sucker!

She cursed Akhil again and tried to peep through the small opening of Nagar's kitchen window. All she could see was a pair of tied hands and the sound of someone weeping badly. She creaked open the window to get a better view.

Holy shit! Is that the saint who just visited them to do some rituals… rituals that would give him a son?

Oh, come on!

Her internal voice echoed while trying to internalize the incident that was taking place inside that house.

Abha tugged her fingers on the side of the kitchen door and pulled it softly. She checked her pocket and cursed herself for leaving her phone next to the television. The door opened effortlessly. She tiptoed in. A mild noise from stumbling onto the mud pot kept at the corner of the kitchen startled her, but the grating sound from the old fan overshadowed the noise. Through the keyhole, she could see all that was happening in their living room.

That fraud man was trying to rob them. His fingers held a sharp knife poised high as he threatened Mr. Nagar. With obscene language coming out of his mouth and a drooling look at Tina, he looked scary. He captured Tina in one hand. His hand rubbed her chest weirdly, making the kid freak out in fear. Mr. Nagar and his wife on their knees begged him to free their daughter then, but his merciless smile and nonstop profanity scared the hell out of them. His fake hair was on the floor, exposing his real hair. He was partially bald with a patch of thin hair combed from one side of his head.

"Please let my daughter go!" Mr. Nagar cried, sitting in one corner. His hands rubbed his moist eyes. The parents looked terrified and numb in fear.

"You decide, money or this girl!" The fraud baba chuckled. His false beard hung from one of the chairs at their dining table.

She stood in the kitchen for a minute, trying to think of a way to chase that fraud guy out, and then suddenly she came up with an idea.

"Hey, hands up!" she kicked opened the door and poised a small revolver at the fraud saint.

The guy panicked in a second. "Who the hell are you?" his body shook in fear seeing a gun in Abha's hand. Tina escaped from his grip and rushed to her mom, frail and frightened.

"Drop your knife, you moron! And leave the house at once!" she commanded. A strange confidence glowed in her eyes and strength on her face.

Mr. Nagar gaped at her with shock, wondering how she managed to come through the balcony. Tears rolled down the mother's eyes when she hugged Tina, hiding her almost inside her saree.

The guy looked at her angrily and tried to find a prop to attack Abha when she pulled the trigger.

"No… wait… I'm leaving! Don't shoot!" he cried this time. His legs shivered, and he stepped back toward the door.

"Take a picture of this fraud!" Abha's voice shot high.

"No… no madam. Please! I beg you!" He cried. "I have a family, and I don't want to go to jail! Please!"

Mr. Nagar scrambled for his phone and captured his pic when the fraud man partly covered his face.

"I'm going!" The man opened the latch and rushed out of their house when Tina's father ran to close the door.

Mr. Nagar walked back and sat at the dining table, his body shivered in fear and distress.

"Thank you so much for saving us!" his gaze down, tears rolling down his eyes.

"Aunty, you have a gun?" His daughter asked, pointing her finger to the revolver Abha was holding. Her mom was still crying, holding her daughter close to her chest.

Abha winked at her. "It's a lighter!" she pulled the trigger again, and a click sound lit the flame.

She thanked Khushi internally for gifting her that antique lighter from her trip to Goa.

Tina's mother gaped at her, and Mr. Nagar's speechless expression looked frame-worthy. Tina's face displayed a naïve smile.

Abha smiled and walked out of their house, and since fortunately her main door was ajar, she didn't have to come back via the same way she entered their house.

"Thank you very much!" a chorus voice followed her way as she closed her door.

She smiled.

After coming back home, her mind now started to process those messages again.

How could he record their intimate moments?

She dialed his number, but it was non-reachable. She screamed in anger. Her angry mind wanted to chuck the phone hard on the floor, but she was a very practical woman and wanted to find a rational solution to this nasty problem.

She planned to walk till Akhil's flat. So she slipped into her flip-flop and grabbed her black stole from the couch. Her neighbor Mr. Nagar was still standing frozen at their door. Tina waved at her from their living room as she got into the elevator.

Chapter 6

After ringing his doorbell about five times and waiting at his doorstep for more than fifteen minutes, an old lady opened the door. She claimed to be Akhil's grandmother.

"He's gone to Bangalore with friends and will be back after a week only!" She said, coughing intermittently.

"Thank you!" Abha said crisply while cursing him internally. The lady slammed the door to close while she was still standing there.

Abha climbed back to her house and tried to notice the number that had just sent her the video. She dialed the number, but it came as switched off. That number was a different number than Akhil's usual number, which raised a little doubt in her mind.

Or is it someone else? A confused voice echoed within her inner conscience.

But how is it even possible? How could someone record an incident that just happened inside my house, behind the closed door?

Her mind went back to Akhil. She just wanted to get hold of him and ask why he had acted so cheaply by recording their intimate video.

A week later:

“May I come in?” Abha followed the nurse to the office of Dr. Karthik.

“Sure. Please come in!” He ushered her in. Another good-looking nurse wearing a neat uniform and probably in her twenties walked out of his room smoothly with a soothing smile on her face.

Looks like the doctor is having a good time here!

Abha’s inner being chuckled.

“So, how’s your cough now? Any discomfort or fatigue?” he tore open something that seemed like a long cotton bud from a plastic packaging.

“Mild but persisting.” Abha replied.

“Let’s do a swab test to rule out few things.” He asked to open her mouth wide.

“Wider please...” He said, which triggered an instant laugh from the nurse.

“What?” he abruptly stopped and stared at her. “Funny?”

“Nothing Doc!”

She gazed down and handed over Abha’s Tod test reports to him and left his chamber quietly.

“Does my report look alright?” Abha asked, thinking about how good or bad the life of a doctor would be.

“Absolutely! And you don’t have sleep apnea, which is great! But mild ADD symptoms are there. I will prescribe you a med which you need to take once daily before your breakfast." He scribbled something on his writing pad.

"Sure!" Abha asserted.

"Was it your dream to be a doctor?" Abha casually asked him.

"Yes and no both. My family is full of doctors, so it's kind of a legacy!" He smiled. "We doctors hardly have a personal life, you know!" He raised one eyebrow in a funny way.

"Sorry if I've asked a wrong question!" She said, seeing him thoughtful.

"Not at all… I am a proud doctor!" He winked and then his eyes went back to reading her reports.

"By the way, I have a question for you. May I?" asked Dr. Karthik.

"Please!" Abha kept her phone aside.

"Do you have a boyfriend?" His gaze dissolved Abha into laughter.

"What do you think?" She said, giggling.

"I think, yes!" He handed over the reports to another nurse and asked her to get a copy of those for their record purpose.

"Are you married?" she asked, grabbing her bag.

"Smart girl!" he said with a smirk.

Abha got up and reached out to shake his hand. His hand lingered a while which gave a strange feeling to Abha. She smiled and he smiled too, their eyes locking each other's for a couple of seconds.

"By the way, I'm not married! And I asked the question on a serious note!" Dr. Karthik replied when Abha was about to leave his chamber.

"Hmm!" Abha blushed, acted no less flirtatious than him. She pulled the door to close on her way out.

It had been a week, and Abha waited for Akhil desperately. She tried calling him multiple times, but none were picked up.

A quick run in the park and after a couple of minutes of small talk with Mr. Ghosh, Abha sat in the quietness of the park. The tranquility of the greenery mixed with the chirping of birds smoothened her restless mind. Her eyes shuffled through the video again when another message made its way.

"Hey beautiful!"

It's the same number again. The number from where the video was sent.

"You moron! Where are you hiding? In Bangalore? But I've never expected that from you!" Abha's message triggered a reply.

"Bangalore? I'm right next to you!" that message puzzled her. She freaked out and leaped to her feet, looking around.

Only Mr. Ghosh and a couple of other elderly men walked in the park.

Is it Mr. Ghosh then? But how would he record what was happening inside my house?

She could not locate any suspicious face even after looking around for minutes. Abha walked to her apartment mindlessly when Mr. Ghosh waved at her but got no response from her.

She briskly walked into her apartment after checking Akhil's flat again. His grandmother creaked open the door, said that he would be back the next day. She could sniff an aroma from their kitchen which made her hungry almost instantly.

The next day:

"How are you, sleeping beauty?" The message on her phone woke her up with a sheer shock, and Abha sprang up from her bed. She felt as if someone was watching her sleeping. Beads of sweat on her forehead, she tied the knot of the robe yet tighter, clutching her slender body. Frisking her hair tying into a messy bun, she read the message yet again. Her mind fumed.

"Akhil, do you think you can scare me with that one video?" She replied angrily, sitting back on the bed again.

Priya called out from the kitchen after preparing coffee for Abha, "Biscuits didi?"

"Yes, please!" Abha sounded a little edgy without her knowledge.

Priya walked to the bedroom with the mug full of coffee and a transparent jar full of thick round bakery biscuits.

Abha picked one from there. Generally, she would smile at Priya and talk for a minute or two when Priya comes with coffee, but that day she didn't bother. Priya stood for a couple of seconds and then scurried back to the kitchen, seeing Abha's not so nice mood. An aroma of raw garlic trailed her way.

"Who said I am Akhil? By the way, I must say that you are hot!" the message shocked Abha, freaking her out to a different level altogether. Abha's ears were fuming, and her heart palpitated in fright.

She couldn't think of anyone else who could take that kind of a video. She had hardly invited anyone after moving to that apartment. She combed through her hair, messing up her already messy curls.

"Who are you and what do you want?" Her straight question did not get a reply, and Abha dropped her phone between her pillows in frustration and walked to the balcony, taking a sip from her extra caffeinated coffee.

Who the fuck could this be if not Akhil?

Her mind went through all the people she had met after she got to Delhi - important, unimportant, small, big, everything. Her fingers started counting the numbers when Susheela interrupted her.

"The sink is leaking water… we need to call the plumber!" Susheela looked half soaked probably after cleaning the overflowed sink.

Abha nodded in agreement, still thoughtful. Susheela strode to the telephone in the living room.

Mr. Ghosh, her jogging partner, Phillip, her boss; Her neighbor Mr. Nagar, Akhil, her doctor, Karthik, the jovial shopkeeper and his boys, her maids, and all the other people whom she saw almost daily or occasionally flashed in front of her eyes again and again. She tried to find any clue from them, from their expressions, anything odd from their behavior. But failed to get a slightest indication of anything being off.

Akhil's face flashed in front of her eyes a couple of times. The warmth that they shared at the nook of her house gave her goosebumps.

Does that mean Akhil is innocent? She walked into her bedroom, and Susheela followed.

Susheela stared at her while tidying up the room.

Could it be the man who came on the other day to rob Mr. Nagar?

Her mind tried to visualize his face with a beard and again without a beard. But she could hardly recollect his face, save for his extra hairy thick eyebrows and his big bulging eyes.

But then she remembered that she had been getting these messages much before she saw that fake saint. So she ruled him out.

A message beeped again as she scrambled through the pile of clothes that Susheela just dumped on the bed for folding. She looked for her favorite pink socks. The weather started to get chillier than usual.

"I can give you a clue!" A message flashed bright on her locked screen. She swiped up her finger to unlock it.

Is this a bloody game!

She wondered, thinking what she should do about that situation. Her fingers hesitated to type anything. She was desperate to know who sent her the video. She was dying to know his identity.

"What's the clue?" she wanted to stay calm. Her only aim was to find the identity of that person.

Abha responded to his message. Her mind started thinking if she should have gone to the police and reported the whole incident. But she was kind of skeptical about doing it. Already the whole Delhi matter was not going well with her parents as well as Animesh, and on top of that, the video was a sex video. She could no way share that with Animesh or with her parents. Her hand went to the phone again, unlocking it again, seeking a reply from the unknown sender. Her sullen face rested in the palm of her hand as she looked out the window. A few kids stood in front of the main entrance for their school bus. Their parents, mainly mothers, accompanied them holding their bags and water bottles.

The security Satish walked past the gate looking up for a moment which gave an instant weirdness to Abha.

What about this man? He was acting funny on the other day!

Abha tried to see where he was going. But he just got vanished walking into the parking at the society's basement.

A few more minutes and her phone beeped again.

"A piece of cake!"

What? A piece of cake? What kind of clue is that?

Abha's eyes rolled from side to side; she tried to give it a think. "A piece of cake" sounded familiar to her as if she had heard someone telling it to her recently.

But who?

Her phone rang out, and her mind had to pause, internalizing that it was getting way too late for the office.

"Hey, Khushi, I'll call you in a bit! We need to talk!" She hung up, grabbed her towel, and rushed to the shower. Arvind, the plumber, after having fixed the sink, walked out in careful steps and closed the main door on his way out.

Chapter 7

"Hey, Abha! So what was it you wanted to talk about?" Khushi's curious voice traveled to her eardrums. His voice was loud enough to reach the Uber driver's ears.

"It's weird, but someone's been messaging me from the last couple of weeks..." Abha said that like an unfinished sentence. The driver took a peek at Abha through the rearview mirror, thinking of an interesting story coming along. She caught his eyes but ignored and kept talking about the messages that she received in the last couple of weeks. Her voice went more subdued than before.

"So, you're telling that you had sex with the guy you just met inside the elevator? And someone took a video of it?" Khushi's virtual gaping face appeared in front of Abha's eyes.

"Please lower your voice, Khushi! And it's not like that. I've known him for some time now!" Abha said, justifying her intimacy with Akhil.

"Hmm...and what about Animesh? Are you guys still together?" Khushi's query sidetracked the whole thing. Abha became thoughtful, a little confused if she really was in love with Animesh.

"Come on, Khushi! Please let's try focusing on this unknown number for now!" She adjusted her shirt buttons as the driver's eyes hovered on her exposed skin.

"You are right! Do you wanna log a complaint at the police station? I think that would be the best option. Leave the search thing to them!" It was not that Abha wasn't thinking about that option, but she kept that as the last weapon.

Khushi further added, "Also, if the person says that he isn't Akhil, then how did the video reach him? This is a pretty serious matter, Abha, and you will have to be extremely careful. Why don't you come and stay in my house for some time?"

"Come on, your house is so far!" Abha's agitated voice shot up. Her fingers ran through combing her hair in a messy way. The driver kept enjoying the story and smirked periodically. It definitely made his day.

They tried to analyze the phrase "A piece of cake" as Abha recalled all the possible people she met after moving to Delhi, and both Khushi and Abha jointly tried to narrow down the puzzle, going to the apparently deepest level with all the clues that were visible to them.

Many names came up starting from the security guard, the fraud man who tried to rob her neighbor, her doctor, the jogger, her neighbor, Akhil, and other people whom she met daily, who came across her way almost every other day or pretty regularly. But they failed to solve the mystery of the "A piece of cake" thing.

"Do you think it could be Animesh himself?" Khushi's voice stabbed her like a sharp knife.

"What? But how? How would he record a video? Does that mean Akhil knows him or is he helping him to a crime?"

Abha felt like the assistant detective from her favorite Sherlock Holmes story.

"There must be a hidden camera in your house, Abha!" Khushi almost whispered.

"Fuck! A piece of Cake? What kind of camera could this be?" Abha reached her destination and hung up the call and exited the car thoughtfully thinking about the chances of having a camera in her house.

Her bouncy curly hair and neatly tucked white shirt on blue jeans caught a couple of eyes, including Phillip's.

"Hey, up for a coffee this evening?" His voice came aloud from the vending machine nook. The receptionist, who was eager to go on a date with Phillip, rolled her eyes in envy. An asymmetrical smile brushed through her lips when she greeted Abha at the reception.

"Thanks for the offer, Phillip! But I already have a date this evening!" Abha said, wanting to avoid any new confusions. Her neatly set teeth flashed a beautiful smile that raised Phillip's eyebrow.

"How sad!" The receptionist's remark agitated him as he walked back to his office after sparing her an angry look.

The whole day, Abha kept thinking about the phrase "A piece of cake" and tried to find to get to the person who was invading her privacy, taking her video and sending her strange messages.

On the way back home, she was desperate to get home and check her house for any hidden camera. Mr. Ghosh waved at her from the park, and she had to stop to talk to him for a few minutes.

"Where are you, young lady?" His jovial voice traveled from the park and made her smile.

"Hi, Mr. Ghosh! You carry on today, and I won't be able to join you this evening!" She came and stood at the other side of the fence, looking at Mr. Ghosh with his dog Rambo and his grandson Arko. He looked a little weak that day and hunched a little more while walking. An awful feeling of getting aged brushed through her mind.

"It's alright! Enjoy your evening, my dear, and don't forget about the marathon event. That's coming up soon!" He said in a demanding tone which felt pretty cute to Abha, and she nodded, smiling back to him.

A car and the person sitting behind the wheel caught her attention and instantly reminded her that she was supposed to go for an early dinner with her doctor. Dr. Karthik asked her out the previous week, and she agreed.

Oh no!

"Hey, when did you come?" Abha halted right in front of her gate, by Karthik's luxury car as he slid down the window shield.

"It's been a couple of minutes. I was just watching you talk to the elderly person in the park. Do you want to join or need a couple of minutes to be ready?" Karthik's polished soothing voice felt a little flirtatious.

"By the way, you look beautiful!" He further uttered, locking her eyes in a romantic way.

"If you could give me ten minutes, it would be great!" Abha looked at her clumsy clothes and undone hair. Her fingers rested on the sleek window of his luxury car.

"Sure, I'll wait for you!" He said politely. "But don't be late, please!" he requested Abha.

The security guard walked past the car yet again with curious eyes, as Abha didn't want to make him wait for long.

After about seven minutes, she was back in a navy blue maxi dress with sleek golden ensembles. Her curly hair looked gorgeous. Smoky eyes and nude lipstick made her stark features a sight to behold. She slid into the car, and slowly the car vanished from sight after catching a few overenthusiastic eyes.

The club with live music and a bar, at a reasonable distance from Abha's house, had a beautiful theme from the 70's Hindi classics. Karthik opened the door and ushered Abha to get into the spacious expanse of the upscale bar. Abha liked his polished behavior. She smiled, taking her steps into the beauty of the ambience. Karthik pulled the chair for Abha and ushered her to sit, then went around the table and sat opposite Abha, flashing a warm smile at her. His extra-nice behavior was not strange to her, but she was more into the casual lifestyle, and his way-too-polished gestures made her a bit conscious. Her mind felt refreshed from the rest of her day-to-day chaos as her eyes went to the singer who was doing a live performance. Even though the songs were from the golden era, the singer flaunted a beaded ponytail and played an acoustic guitar. He modified each song and presented them in a more soothing note, more suitable for a tranquil surrounding. In the back of her mind, she thought about those strange messages. The bold video, which brought back the time that she spent with Akhil on her couch, made her sulk. Even though the quality of the video was poor, it wouldn't be difficult to say that the girl in the video was Abha. Her eyebrows cringed without her knowledge.

"Hey! All okay?" Karthik gave her hand a friendly shake.

"Of course! Everything is fine! The wine is tangy though!" Abha drummed up a false explanation, justifying her lost expressions.

"Don't force it then, let's order something else than." He waved at a waiter.

Karthik's sober nature, his graceful talk, and a charming smile felt serene to Abha. He seemed like a pure gentleman to her. His open-button blazer over a white shirt gave him a subtle look. Her sheath dress with delicate ensembles made her look a little different than her usual self.

"I'd like to know more about you!" Karthik looked into her eyes, not like a doctor but like someone who might be looking for more than just a friend.

"You have all my reports!" Abha smirked, tucking her curly bangs behind her ear.

"Smart girl!" He smiled. "But my report doesn't verify if you have a boyfriend or not!"

They both broke into a giggle.

The lights went dim as more couples joined the dance floor. They mostly did slow moves as the songs were suitable only for lazy legs.

"Dance!" He moved his chair and got to his feet in a yet dramatic posture. "Will you dance with me?" His hand extended to Abha, ready to pull her into an intimate move. "No...!" Abha raised her eyebrows, her eyes rounder than ever. She giggled. "Sit down!" She pulled his hand and made him sit again, next to her this time, his hand touching and overlapping Abha's fingers every now and then. She didn't miss to realize that Karthik was very much attracted to her.

After a couple of drinks and yummy grilled kebabs and pleasant live music, Abha's mind felt relaxed, and the strange messages that were clogging her brain took a sideline.

"I know it's not a date night, but how about me asking you a direct question?" Dr. Karthik sounded more serious this time. His fingers rubbed the surface of her fingers.

"Sure!" Abha took yet another sip from her Merlot. Her eyes drifted to Karthik's hand that was interlacing her fingers, which made him blush.

"Do you like me?" He winked. "Do I even hold a chance?"

"What kind of chance?" Abha spared a confused smile.

"Umm... maybe a chance to be your life-partner? Because I think, I started to like you a lot!" The other hand layered Abha's hand making a soft clutch. His eyes sincere.

"Karthik... let's give it some more time, please! You're undoubtedly a beautiful person but let's not hurry things up." Abha smiled. The curls of her hair went about her face when someone turned on the huge antique fan that kept at the nook.

“Sure! Take your time!” Karthik loosened his grip. His fingers curled back into a soft fist.

After a fine dinner and comfortable chatting, Abha and Karthik walked back to the parking lot. He offered her a smoke, and she took it.

“I didn’t know that you smoke!” She gave him a surprised look.

“I’ve got it for you… thought you might like it!” Lady, I did enough research on your reports, you must say!” yet another blush on Karthik’s face. “Btw, your vitals look fine, and you can smoke, but being a doctor, I must not encourage it down the line!” He announced. “Yes, Doc!” Abha dissolved into a giggle.

A piece of cake!

Abha’s mind dove into deep thought and failed to notice that Karthik had already parked his car a little short of the entrance of her society.

“So when are we meeting again?” his hand took Abha’s hand, fondling her fingers in a coquettish way.

“Soon!” Abha replied.

“Is something bothering you? Is it me?” He asked, pursing his lips.

“No, no, no…!” She clutched his hand. “I’ve a follow-up appointment with you next week! But if you want, we could meet sooner as well!” Abha sounded cheerful.

“Hmm…that’s alright! You take your time.” His relaxed voice conveyed.

"Thanks for the beautiful evening!" Abha's gaze at Karthik was intoxicating. The kohl-rimmed eyes smeared the kohl a little outside the borderline. He rubbed his thumb along the line and smudged it, giving her a mild churn in her stomach. A sensuous feeling ran down her nerves, traveling to her lower abdomen. "Thanks, Karthik!" First time she took his name. He blushed. She closed her eyes. There was a blush at the corner of her lips. When Karthik leaned further on her side, she moved a bit further. The strap of her dress fell off her shoulder. His nose skimming her shoulder inhaling deep, made a way to her earlobe. His musky fragrance felt warm when he kissed her shoulder. Abha bit her lips with a soft moan, heat building up in her core when Karthik's lip whispered Love you in her ears. He came closer almost diminishing the gap between them. Abha ran her fingers brushing his soft tufts pulling him closer. Karthik sucked in her lips and a wild romance broke out instantly. "No..." a soft escaped from her mouth. His fingers slipped down her silky top made its way to the hook of her corset. Abha moaned, her body shivered, breath rapid. But suddenly a huge thudding noise startled them both. It came like as if something tried to smash something on his car.

"Shit!" Abha startled adjusting her top.

"Calm down! It's alright!" Karthik took a peek at the almost empty road. A bike looked to speed up fast and vanished taking a right turn at the end of the dead end.

"What was it?" Abha stared at Karthik, perplexed.

"Let me check!" He opened the door and tried to check the side of the car. Nothing much was visible due to the darkness of the secluded edge of the road except a small dent and a scratch on the car.

He got back into the car and started the vehicle.

“Is there any damage?” Abha raised her eyebrows in concern.

“A little, don’t worry, I’ll get it fixed tomorrow!” He said but soberly.

“I’m sorry!” She uttered, her face sad.

“Why are you saying sorry? It’s not your fault!” Karthik glanced at her, his eyes mainly on the road. His hand gave a gentle rub on her thigh.

Are these two things related? The message and this weird incident of somebody dashing his car?

The car stopped in front of her society gate and she got off and sent him off with a smiling yet pale face.

“Cheer up!” He waved at her, and Abha, flashing a smile again, walked toward the elevator fearing if anyone was following her.

Chapter 8

Night at 1 AM:

Abha stood right at the dining table and gaped at the wall clock that was ticking away time matching her heartbeats. The clock had a strange antique shape which looked like a piece of a metal pizza or like a piece of cake with one slice little off from the rest of the base.

Holy Cow! It's a piece of cake!

Her internal voice echoed in her mind. She walked around the table trying to recollect the moment when Animesh gifted her the clock. The day when they went out to a small-scale antique shop in order to look for a nested table for Abha. They failed to get a good table, but Animesh picked up the wall clock since Abha brushed her fingers on it each time she crossed the wall. She was very touched by Animesh's gesture and fell a little more for him from that day. She narrowed her eyes and cringed her brows again coming back to the present.

Come on, Animesh! You didn't have to play so cheap!

With Abha's frustration shooting up, she moved the dining table a bit from the wall and shoved in a stool there to get that clock down.

Is there a camera inserted somewhere inside the clock? Does Animesh have a dark side that he just kept to himself?

A sheer sense of fear ran down her nerves, throttling her throat.

Is he seeing me right now? No, it's late, and he must be sleeping!

Abha took the clock down. It collected some dust in a couple of months. As her fingers brushed the rim of it, a layer of dirt smudged her hand. She pulled the kitchen towel and wiped it and finally sat on the couch with the clock on her lap. The angle of the clock appeared right if somebody wanted to capture the happenings on the couch.

She flipped it sideways and front and back, shook it real hard when a sound as if something moved inside the clock got her attention. She moved her hand on the clock surface when a small button-like thing which looked like a piece of a broken button came into her hand. It was very tiny but looked like a round frame and had some lenses inside.

Fuck! This looks like a camera! Shit! Does that mean Animesh has been stalking me?

Abha's face went red in anger as she dropped the clock on the center table with a clatter. Her phone showed 1.45 AM, and she punched in Animesh's number hastily, ready to charge him for his nasty perverted deed.

"Hello…" a subdued drawl came from the other side of the line. Aninmesh's sleepy voice came yet concerned with Abha's late-night call.

"Is everything ok? Why are you calling me this late?" This time the voice picked a mild pitch.

"You tell me, Animesh! Is everything alright with you?" Her edgy voice irked him.

"What do you mean? Did you call me to ask for this in the middle of the night, waking me up from a deep sleep?" Animesh's eyes droopy in sleep, mind refused processing anything.

"Why the fuck have you implanted a camera in my clock? You are invading my privacy, and I'll never forgive you for that!" Abha's high pitch shirk echoed in the vestibule.

"What do you mean? What camera? What are you talking about?" Animesh rubbed his eyes scratching his messed-up hair.

"Oh yeah! Come on, you can do better acting, dude!" Abha threw the clock once again on the floor, making a bad sound which could wake up the people living downstairs.

"You can't talk to me like that, Abha! I'm hanging up if you keep talking nonsense like this!"

Abha tried to compose herself. She lit a smoke and strode to the balcony. Everything felt tranquil and ghostly with some on and off sounds of car horns in the middle of the night.

"Ok..." She breathed in. "Why did you hide a fucking camera inside the clock you gifted me? Are you trying to bloody stalk me?" Abha's talk sounded absolutely strange to Animesh.

"Because I never did that, Abha! What will I gain doing so? And what's happening there? What camera... what clock? Please tell me properly what happened?" Animesh sounded extremely concerned and all ears to listen to Abha.

She skipped the Akhil part and told the rest of the story stating that somebody had been trying to record her through the camera.

"I think you will have to be very careful and report this to the police at once! Can I call my uncle? You know he's a DIG right?" Animesh's concern made her almost numb. The absolute feeling of something scary haunted her. She walked back and locked the balcony door and pulled the mesh and curtain and walked to the other rooms to check the doors and windows.

"I'll call you later!" Abha sounded low with tears touching the brim of her eyes.

"I'm coming tomorrow, and we'll..." Animesh's half-ended statement got overlapped by the beeping sound as Abha disconnected the phone and slumped down on the sofa, frustrated and scared. Early morning birds started chirping slowly drifting her off to sleep.

Next day:

The doorbell rang multiple times waking her up from a deep sleep. Abha opened the door, and Arvind, the plumber person, walked in after a quick greeting to Abha. Followed him walked in her maid Susheela and Priya.

She rubbed her eyes looking at the clock which was not hung on that wall anymore.

Sucks!

"What's the time?" Abha checked her phone, which was switched off.

"We've been waiting here for an hour now! I also knocked the door at 6 am, but no one responded, so I thought you must be sleeping." Susheela said with a little agitated voice walking into the bathroom with the hamper to get the clothes soaked. Priya followed Susheela without saying anything, and Arvind removed his shoes and wore a liner before walking to the kitchen side balcony in with his tool box.

"Are you doing some kind of repair today?" Abha uttered, a little bit vexed with his almost daily visits.

"Yes, madam. The drainage pipe needs to be replaced in all the flats. They are causing water leakage on the main." He looked up at Abha for the first time. Abha noticed that he had innocent big eyes and a stark face. He walked with a straight face and vanished into the balcony next to the kitchen.

Abha exhaled a deep sigh and sat on the sofa curling in her legs and changed the channels. Cooking sounds, cleaning noises, and the washing machine sound overshadowed the TV sound, and she stretched her limbs and laid down on the sofa once again thinking about strange happenings.

Animesh called up, but she ignored. She muted the phone, switched off the TV. Her brain pushed her to a deep sleep again.

11 o'clock, Susheela woke her asking her to close the door since they were done for the day. Chicken was prepared and kept decoratively on the dining table with rice and eggplant fry. The house looked neat and clean, refreshed with rose-hinted Lysol. But the clock looked to be missing from the chair.

Susheela must have taken it for cleaning!

She locked the door after they left and walked to the dining nook to check on the clock. It was not there as well. Arvind's shoes looked to be missing which made it clear that he must have left when she was asleep. Abha got rid of her last night's old T-shirt and shorts. Her nude body stood in front of the mirror as her fingers brushed through her curves. She changed into a maxi skirt and a black tank top and skipped wearing a bra. The skin between the top and skirt looked attractive. A sound from the bedroom caught her attention. It sounded like a closet closing sound. Her heart skipped a beat. Her curiosity shot mixed with fear, and she maneuvered through the buckets and hampers to her bedroom.

"Trr....ing!" The doorbell diverted her from going into the room, and she walked to the main door instead.

It was Akhil standing with a small box that looked to be a present, probably for Abha from Bangalore, wrapped with some blue glittering paper.

"Akhil!" Abha murmured. She felt embarrassed for her no-bra attire.

"Hey! I am sorry! I was off to meet my grandfather. He wasn't keeping well these days and had to be admitted to the hospital. Sorry, I couldn't inform you!" He removed his shoes and placed them neatly at the corner of Abha's door and took a step ahead to enter when Abha's hand stopped him, blocking him from entering into her house.

"Hey..." Akhil looked at her.

"Please leave! I'm definitely not in a mood to talk to you. I'd been looking for you like crazy since weeks and now you are showing up from out of the blue with a present in hand? I definitely don't want you in my life! Please leave, Akhil." Her hand still strongly blocking his way from entering her flat.

"Come on, Abha! I said I'm sorry! It won't happen again!" He pledged. His eyes locking Abha's. But she broke off the gaze.

"You're an immature kid! And this isn't going to work out! Please leave!" Abha's further aggression pointed him to the elevator. Mr. Nagar spared both of them a suspicious look when he came to grab the newspaper from the front of his door. He walked back in but left his door open which led both Abha and Akhil a little uncomfortable.

"Abha, please!" Akhil mouthed, making a pitiful face.

"Ok, but let's talk later!" Abha said with a straight face.

"Ok. I'll be waiting at the apartment coffee shop at 5 PM!" Akhil left taking the steps back, handing her the small box that he got for Abha. And Before Abha could say anything, he walked down.

Abha slammed the door and opened the fancy ribbon that was tied, or might be just attached, on the top of the box. She yanked open the box revealing a beautiful velvety glittery case. It had a small lock which could be flipped open.

Another sound from the bedroom diverted her yet again. She dropped the box on the corner of the dining table and tiptoed to her bedroom. Everything looked perfect, except some rings of smoke exiting from the balcony.

"Arvind, What are you doing here? I thought you were done?" Abha got a shock of her life when she saw Arvind, her plumber, fixing something sitting at the nook of her balcony adjacent to the kitchen. The clock that she left on the chair was in his hand. Tiny particles sprawled surrounding the clock while he was engrossed tightening with screws. He had a cigarette poised between his fingers. When she felt that it had the same menthol smell, she found her packet of cigarettes next to his tool bag.

"What's going on?" Abha swallowed a scream. "Did you do that?" her voice murmured but nothing came out of her lungs. As if someone was choking her breath. As if there was a big rock standing on her chest.

"You shouldn't have pulled the clock off! I was having a good time!" He chuckled, got to his feet, his eyes were big, and there was no mask on his face. Instead, his flaunted smile was mischievous, evil.

"What do you mean?" Abha stepped back as his hand approached to catch her arm. It was the first time Abha saw his face. His stark face had big eyes and fuller lips. His teeth were not aligned properly and partly blackened, mostly due to smoking.

"Don't touch me!" Abha batted Arvind's hand, looking at him with sheer disgust.

The weather was getting gloomy with a hint of rain in the clouds. The rest of the windows and doors were shut. She wanted to rush back and close the balcony door, locking him out, but instead, due to panicking, she stumbled on the wet broomstick and bucket and slipped and fell on the kitchen floor. That gave extra time to Arvind to easily squeeze into her kitchen. He latched the door from inside.

Abha rushed to the door to check if she could get hold of her neighbor or Akhil, but he ran faster and wrapped her from the back and literally dumped her on the bed. He chuckled in a wicked way. His eyes were calm, but there was a storm of agony, a strange craving.

"Don't do anything foolish, I say! You will have to repent for it!" She stared at Arvind. His eyes looked different, as if it was altogether a new person, or maybe Abha had never tried to notice his face or, for that matter, anything about him.

"Remove it!" He ordered, eyeing her top. He bit his lips in a disgusting way that gave goosebumps to Abha.

"No bra…" he winked. His eyes scanned her breasts like an x-ray machine. The same bad smile lingered on his lips.

"Help!" she rushed to the balcony, but his approach scared her. There was a tiny knife in his hand. She slowly walked back in. Arvind came closer, and a strange smell of sweat almost gave a feeling of nausea to Abha. She shivered in fear. His fingers brushed through the skin of her arm, and suddenly he pinned her against the wall. His arms layered her neck firmly, locking her into that position.

"What do you want?" She faltered.

His one finger moved on her shoulder, untying the knot of one side of her tank top. The untied lace moved the neckline of the top further down, exposing most of her breasts.

"Please… no. I'll give you money!" Abha's hand clutched her top as he chuckled cunningly. "Who wants it?"

"Listen, even I don't want to force anything on you. But I'm hardly able to resist me here, and you need to help me out. Whatever you've done with Akhil on that couch, do the same and I'll leave." He sat on the bed lighting another smoke. "So remove it!" He ordered again.

"And if I don't?" Abha tried to move sideways toward the kitchen, but Arvind's eyes indicated her to stay in place. "Remove it, Bitch!" he screamed.

She removed the other knot. Her top fell helplessly on the floor, exposing her in breast and shorts. He came closer, his eyes lustfully scanning through Abha's body. "Ahh! What a sight!"

Abha rushed to the vestibule, "Help! Help!" but Arvind came right behind, chasing her, and closed her mouth. Both wrestled along the dining table, with Abha trying hard to get rid of his grip. The bowls kept on the dining table jiggled, sliding the lids from them. Abha already felt exhausted since no proper food from last night and a mild hangover from the alcohol. She cried for help yet again. Her ribs hurt from Arvind's grip. She tried to make maximum noise, but Arvind dragged her to the bedroom, pushing her again onto the bed. He got some tool out of his box, which looked like a screwdriver but had a slightly different shape. Abha kept mum, tears rolling down her eyes. He grabbed her feet and slowly slid his hand beneath her shorts, frisking the skin of her left thigh, making his way higher each time. Her nipples hardened. The sharp tool was poised to Abha, kept her frozen and immovable. His moist tongue rolled on her breasts. "She screamed "No!" but he hardly bothered. Her eyes rolled sideways, searching for something with which she could smash his head. The table clock grabbed her attention, but it seemed to have a low impact if someone were hurt with it. Still, something is better than nothing. She breathed in softly to stay calm when Arvind felt a little strange due to the sudden pause in her restlessness. He looked around and pushed the clock with a chuckle.

"I'm not a fool, you beautiful lady!" he came closer, moving his mouth to her lips. His hand went to her back, grabbing her the tightest. She kicked her legs and hands, but he was literally sitting on her. Her mouth dried, and she could hardly make any noise. His tongue glided on her lips, giving Abha sheer disgust. She wanted to kick his groin, but for that, he had to loosen his grip. She gathered the courage to find a plan to escape from the demon. His mouth sucked in her mouth, and a moan came loudly from the back of his throat. His grip loosened slightly, and Abha was waiting to grab it. She panicked like hell but didn't lose hope. In a haste, when Arvind unzipped his pants, Abha had the opportunity to loosen her legs. And she was waiting. She kicked his groin as hard as possible, and Arvind screamed and fell on the bed. Abha scrambled up to her feet, clutching onto her top on the way, and ran to the hall breathlessly.

"Help! Please help!" she cried. Her limbs hurt. She covered her chest with the top. But something hit her head hard suddenly, and she fell on the floor. Her nail tried to grab his shirt, but her vision blacked out for a minute.

"You made me do that! I never intended to hurt you!" he sat down next to her. A strong smell of pungent tobacco was prominent from his breath. She tried to welt but failed to fist her palm. She kept looking at Arvind, and his hand went to the zip of her shorts, yanking it open.

"No! Please!" a helpless murmur came out of Abha's mouth.

Arvind's wicked smile flashed brighter. His face came closer to her mouth, and his finger slid through her innerwear, grabbing her tight. Lust was written all over his face as his grip tightened. His rough kisses scarred her skin, and she tried kicking her legs, which had hardly any strength left in them.

A sudden sharp sound pitched up high. It felt to be approaching closer, giving a fearful jitter to Arvind. His eyes blinked, and his hand automatically slid out from underneath her attire. He tried to heed the sound.

It sounded like some kind of alarm or a siren from a police vehicle. Abha's half-conscious ear could hear the same sound and noticed Arvind getting disturbed by that sound.

"Police... Police!" knocks were prominent on the front door.

"Help!" she screamed again, and then a vigorous knocking sound on the door came out strongly, giving her an instant hope. She staggered up to her feet, and Arvind also stood up. His steps went back by a couple of inches, and suddenly he ran to the kitchen balcony to flee. A sudden thudding sound came out right after Arvind tried to escape through the balcony, as if someone jumping off somewhere and falling on a hard surface.

Abha's body ached, and her face hurt from the bang. She clutched a shawl and scrambled to the door and opened it, her eyes blurring out again.

"Mr. Nagar!" she exclaimed; her head was bleeding and vision blurred. She stood partly naked in front of him.

Tears rolled down non-stop seeing Mr. Nagar there.

"It's alright, Abha! I could figure out something wrong inside your house! And your screams…" he gazed down, giving a few minutes to Abha for covering herself.

"Was there a police?" Abha blinked, blood dripping down her eyelids.

"Umm… it was actually me… and that's just my daughter's toy car!" he said.

Even with a lot of pain, Abha had a gleam of laughter on her lips. "Let's go to the hospital first, and we can talk later on this." He punched in some numbers, and Abha crouched down, pressing her wound with the hand towel Mrs. Nagar handed her.

Abha looked at Mr. Nagar, and he nodded and smiled. A sigh of relief brushed through their faces.

Third Story: Fancy a Coffee?

Chapter 1

Year 1999:

It was a sultry day. A sponge of cloud gathered tightly at the northeast corner of the pink sky, perhaps trying to overshadow the glistening rays of the sun. I waited at the overcrowded bus stop near Adyar Ananda Bhavan. Screening the unknown crowd around me, I double-checked the bus number one last time and exhaled a breath of relief as it approached the stop. People had already started rushing toward it, leaving trails of musty sweat in the humid Sunday afternoon.

That bus would take me to my elder sister after a long, tiring, fruitless day, and maybe that would make me less homesick; thoughts ran in my mind.

A dark blue salwar kameez and a white & blue batik dupatta pinned on my shoulders, I chugged up the stairs of the public bus and could make my way somewhat to the middle, pushing through the swarm of people. The seats were occupied. I looked around. An old man sitting on the last row stared at me as if some kind of x-ray machine was fixed in his eyes. "Seriously!" I murmured, moved further. A middle-aged man in a khaki shirt, mostly the conductor of the bus, ushered me to sit on his seat as he manoeuvered through the crowd hollering, "Tickets... tickets" in a hoarse voice. I smiled, thanking him, but he was already gone by then. A long day of practical classes on fluid mechanics was exerting, and hence my head automatically leaned on the pole without my knowledge. Gentle breeze percolated through the fizz of my hair and gave me a soothing feeling. The same person in khaki attire stopped right in front of me, flapping his palm… wanting to know my destination.

"Ticket… ticket… ticket…" He looked around for new commuters.

"Hindustan College…" my voice was more like a mumble, but he probably read my lips and handed me a ticket to Kelambakkam bus stop. I felt embarrassed to have settled on his seat and sprang up instantly, but it looked like he realized the exhaustion on my face. I couldn't understand his language, but the signs indicated me to remain seated, and hence I followed it with a smile, probably with gratitude in my eyes. The day-scholars used to avail the same numbered bus to get to the college on a daily basis, and hence guessing my stop wouldn't have been difficult for him. I clutched onto the ticket and the change. The coins were moist from the sweat of his palm, so was the ticket. I shoved them into the front pocket of my backpack and then looked out the window, scanning through the suburbs. Small shops and marketplaces, fruit shops, roadside potteries made the summer colorful, but there were also lengthy deserted paddy fields. They looked eerie and gave me an unknown fear. It was the first time I was traveling alone on a long-distance commute, in a bus full of unknown people.

My name is Niharika Mohanta, and that Sunday I was going to meet my elder sister Niyati at her hostel. It had been only a couple of months since I came from my hometown.

Niyati didi was pursuing her B.Sc degree at Hindustan Arts and Science College, but for me, my parents had chosen a different college. Even today, after three decades, when I still try to think whether the decision of putting me in a different college was due to their financial constraints or because the college where I got admission was a college exclusively for girls, I still wonder.

More people got into the already packed bus. The sky was getting duskier, and a mild fear crawled into my mind thinking about how to walk the distance from the main entrance of my sister's college campus to her hostel. That was a hell of a stretch, and walking alone would definitely be creepy and of no fun. I remembered the last time an egg-van almost ran over my uncle when he came to drop off Niyati didi at her hostel. He said it was dark, and the driver could hardly see much. It gave me chills. I swallowed my scary thoughts. Niyati didi had insisted many times if she should come and get me from my place, but I was stubborn and assured her that I would reach safe and sound. But when the time came, sitting in a cramped bus facing an unknown crowd, my confidence started to die down.

A group of boys hopped in when I looked at the door blankly. Two boys sat on the second row and a few stood next to them, looking at me curiously on and off. I had never seen them before, but I could hear them talk, and from the conversations, I could realize that they were also talking in Bengali. My mother tongue is Bengali, and hearing them talk in Bengali, my inner mind briefly gained a strange confidence. Their dialect was a little different, but I couldn't clearly hear them due to the rest of the noise in the bus. Their eyes drifted to my side occasionally, and I pretended to be unknown about it, trying to think if I knew any of them, if any face looked familiar.

The distance was long; my sister had already intimated me that the end-to-end journey would take about two hours by bus. Thinking about it, I fished out my Walkman from my not-very-cool backpack and unwrapped the earplugs, shoving them into my ears. I pressed the play button to listen to one of my favorite film songs. My lips synced with the song lyrics, humming them quietly, while my eyes started enjoying the green expanse of the outskirts of the city with a mild worry inside my soul. Someone from that group of boys walked over and stopped right in front of me. His lips moved, and I read "Hello" in them. My eyes broadened, realizing that someone was trying to interact, and I pushed the stop button of my Walkman abruptly.

"Hey, if I'm not wrong, are you Niyati's sister?" That person in his early twenties asked; his hand reached out to hold the pole, and I thought he approached me for a handshake. Then I realized that he did that for balancing as the bus approached a stop. He was of moderate height, with wheatish complexion, and his hair was silky and inky. His fingers combed through his thick black hair, making a back brush. His eyes were small, but there was a strange sparkle of curiosity in them, and he smiled brightly. I noticed his charming smile, and then my eyes turned to his friends who remained at the same spot where they were initially gathered; their curious eyes were glued to us, obviously. It felt pretty awkward.

"Yes," I nodded with a smile. I had to talk a little louder than my usual voice, which strained my throat. I was an extremely quiet teenager. Even the thought that I might have to talk to someone or face someone would make me feel nervous and shy. I was like a little snail who always carried its shell. So obviously, my answer was short.

He smiled, and I mustered up the courage to ask, "How do you know me?"

"One of my friends… looks like he'd seen you with Niyati!" He looked over his shoulder to his friends, but I couldn't figure out whom he was pointing to. His statement sounded more like a question, though.

"Oh!" I smiled. Their eyes were still on me. A face from the same group looked familiar, but then I looked at the sky, and it looked duskier. My core frowned.

"My name is Shamik Roy. Niyati is my senior in college, different department though!" he flashed a smile yet again, and I noticed the captivating gesture of combing his hair yet again. I nodded with acknowledgment.

Can he help me if it gets too dark… like walking till my sister's hostel?

Thoughts ran in my mind.

I was thinking of a way to engage him, and it seemed like even luck favored me as he settled himself next to the pole. The rest of the journey went quickly; we kept conversing, more from his side and a little from mine. After a brief curiosity, even his friends got busy talking among themselves and stopped staring at us. I was a quiet girl, and Shamik figured that out and hence did most of the talking. After an hour and a half, we reached our destination. The inky sky made my heart thump, fearing the fairly long distance to the hostel. I needed to walk and reach there before six. I exhaled a long sigh.

The bus stopped at Kelambakkam.

"Will you be okay? You know where the hostel is, right?" his strong gaze asked me, his eyes had concern in them. His friends walked past us one after another, chugging down the bus stairs. I got down, and he followed. The bus conductor signaled the driver, and the bus started and vanished, blowing a good amount of dust on its way.

"Umm…I should be fine!" I gave a thoughtful answer, but he could figure and measure my fear.

"No… let me come with you!" He smiled, and I felt happy instantly. I blushed, feeling a relief within my core, and thanked him inwardly.

We walked past the canteen, playground, and basketball court, college buildings on the way to the hostel. It was a long way, and the dusky evening crawled into a night sky by the time we reached the hostel gate.

"Here you go!" we stopped, and his eyes moved to the hostel gate.

I could clearly hear girls' voices from the other side of the wall and also noticed his eyes moving to some of the hot-looking, short-dressed college chicks.

"Thank you, Shamik!" I smiled, my hand reached to open the hostel gate.

"Do you have a contact number?" His straightforward question startled me for a moment.

"I stay in my hostel. Do you have a paper?" I asked, rummaging my bag for a pen, anxious.

He extended his palm. "You can write here!" my eyes toggled between his eyes and his palm. He smiled again. I felt hesitant.

Is he trying to flirt?

My fingers grabbed something like a pen from my bag. It was an eyebrow pencil which looked quite similar to a pen in the dark.

"This will do too!" His involuntary words, and I blushed.

We both smirked, avoiding each other's eyes.

I wrote my hostel number on his palm.

"Thanks!" Crisp response from him.

I swallowed a blush and bit my cheek.

"Bye," he stepped back a little and then left briskly, probably to pace up to his friends. I opened the gate and maneuvered through the girls who sat on the stairs, almost blocking my way. They spared me a strange look, and I started looking for my sister's room number. She said she would be busy rehearsing for her upcoming cultural program, but I could knock on her room door, and her roomie Rashmi would be there.

It did happen that way. After finding her room, I knocked, and Rashmi welcomed me with open arms. Her warm smile and soft nature instantly made me comfortable. The room had two metal beds, two sets of study tables and chairs, two shelves, and one cupboard. A good-sized music player was also there, and a large-size mirror also stood slanted at one corner of the room. The temperature inside the room was warmer than usual. I grabbed a change of clothes and my sister's bucket and mug and followed Rashmi as she guided me to the common bathroom. My dusty body needed an urgent shower.

Water streamed through my nerves, relaxing my exhausted limbs. I remembered my conversation with Shamik once again. A smile brushed through my lips. A strange content feeling smoothed my soul. When I was almost done with my shower, a series of rattles on my bathroom door freaked me out.

"Bunu....when did you come?" It almost punched my eardrums.

It was my sister. Her voice echoed loud in that narrow corridor, and I came out wrapped in a skimpy towel and hushed her up.

"Why are you screaming, di?"

I frowned, and she hugged me tight. She had a habit of hugging me tight and kissing my lips each time we met. It annoyed me at times in a funny way. As a big sister, at times she was overprotective of me, and I used to take the privileges of her love.

"I had to come all by myself! You could've come to the gate at least!" I said, sulking my face. "Aww..." I walked to the room, dripping water on the way, and she followed me, grabbing the empty bucket and my wet clothes.

In the room, Rashmi stood ready with a steel plate and glass in her hands, ready to leave, as the dinner bell rang loud at the corner of the corridor. I quickly changed, and Niyatidi grabbed two plates and two glasses, and we made our way to the mess for dinner. I looked around in awe. Everything looked wonderful, grand to me. My hostel was very small compared to her hostel, and their dining room was huge. A huge water filter filled with jeera water was placed at one corner of the hall. All the girls sat in rows, and designated people in uniform came and served food to us. It was a vegetable biryani day. So we got a portion of biryani and two boiled eggs and raita each.

We polished our plates in no time and waited for another portion of biryani.

"Hey, did you meet Shamik?" My sister suddenly asked me.

"What… yeah but how do you know?" *It's not even an hour I met him…*, surprised.

She had a mischievous smile on her face.

"What?" My eyebrows raised, trying to read her eyes.

"Nothing…" She said, smiling.

"No… what is it?" I insisted.

"I have heard that you have given your hostel number to him and…" she handed the jeera water-filled plastic bottle to me.

"Ouch!" The bottle felt soaring hot and softened due to heat. It was not very healthy to fill hot water in regular plastic bottles. But we were never aware of those facts during college days. Rashmi was still waiting in the line to get her bottle filled.

"And?" My eyes questioned, locking di's eyes, trying to know more on the gossip.

"Umm… and instead of using a pen and paper, you have written your number using your lipstick on his palm. I was wondering why…" her brow furrowed, trying to deep think probably.

"Nothing like that!" I instantly replied, but my heart skipped a beat.

Few girls were busy watching a romantic Tamil film at the hostel's recreation hall where, in the film, the hero was busy admiring the heroine's exposed hip. Rashmi abruptly stopped to get a longer view of the scene. And seeing her, even I stopped for a second.

"Arre yaar!" Niyatidi jerked my elbow, and a funny grin brushed through both Rashmi and my face. "Girls! He is not staring at your hips! Let's go to our room, I'm dead tired."

Our innocent yet loud giggle caught a few of the seniors' eyes. Niyatidi hushed us, and then we quietly walked, following a group of Malayali girls and reached our room.

"So? Didn't you have a pen and paper in your bag?" She asked strictly clinging on to the subject as we entered our room. Rashmi didn't have any hint of our conversation, but still a constant smile was pasted on her face each time we shared a look.

Poor thing!

"I couldn't find one in a hurry." My answer short and quiet. "But I haven't used lipstick either. It was just a coal liner…"

my sentence sounded unfinished, and my sister gave a strange nod.

"Bunu, be careful with that boy! He's not right for you!" She said, concerned.

"Come on! I didn't have any other thing in my mind! And it's just a hostel phone number not even a personal number! And you know that my hostel phone remains engaged forever! So it doesn't mean anything…" I reacted suddenly without knowing the reason for my unnecessary defensive answer.

"Hmm… I'm just saying it for your good! He is a little strange, and I think you should stay away from him." She said, just sharing a glance at me. I nodded, thinking what that *strange* meant.

Rashmi took out a cassette from its case and shoved that into the music player. The songs started smoothening three of our minds as we quietly leaned on our respective beds. We enjoyed the divinely beautiful composition of A. R. Rahman. My mind shuffled through the conversations that I had with Shamik yet again.

But why? Why am I thinking about him?

My mind sighed.

Chapter 2

Two months later:

Rupa was busy doing our household chores in the kitchen, and Rashmi was busy working on her assignment sitting at the breakfast nook. I had invested my apparently precious time cleaning the cassette shelf with an old frock of mine, and Niyati di had gone out with her college friends. We had moved into an apartment close to Niyati di's college, and my mother sent Rupa from our hometown to take care of our household needs, mainly cooking.

In those two months, I had never received any call from Shamik. However, it could be because we had left our hostels, and hence he couldn't reach me. It's not that his thought never came to my mind, but my sister's big 'no-no' always stopped me from thinking more.

The doorbell rang. Rashmi was about to get up, but seeing me walk toward the door, she continued with her work, and I went to attend the door.

It was Niyatidi. She was back from a get-together with friends. But it looked like someone was there with her. When he came closer, a bell rang in my head.

Oh! I have seen him somewhere!

"Hey, meet my friend Abhik and Abhik, this is my baby sister Niharika!" Niyatidi gave my cheeks a squeeze, which gave me instant embarrassment. Not again! I eyeballed her, and she, as usual, ignored my expressions. But I didn't miss seeing Abhik's smirk. She ushered him into our living room.

"Hello..." I said. He reached out to shake my hand. "Why does it feel that I have seen you before?" my eyes narrowed.

"Yes..." he smiled. "We met in a bus, but we never spoke with each other though!" he said with a brief smile. His short height, sharp features, and black Metallica t-shirt gave him a spunky look.

"Oh yes, *I remember now!" He was on the same bus, in the same group with Shamik!* I smiled broadly as I followed them to our living room. Yet again the conversation with Shamik ran through my mind.

Abhik sat on one of our red plastic chairs that we had purchased the previous week from a roadside shop. Niyatidi quickly rushed to our common bedroom and came back with a bundle of papers in her hand.

"Here you go." She handed her notes to Abhik.

"Thanks!" his reply was short and crisp. He looked at me and smiled. I smiled back. I could see something beyond a smile in his eyes, as if he was sharing more than just a formal smile, as if his eyes were darkening to lock my eyes.

"I'll take your leave!" Abhik said slipping into his black slippers.

"Bye!" Niyatidi waved and took her steps back into the hall, but I stayed at the doorstep.

When walking down the stairs, Abhik looked over his shoulder. I realized that I was still standing at the door. I bit my lips, embarrassed.

Two weeks later:

We had managed to take a landline connection and finally had the leverage of talking to our parents daily. Rashmi too spoke to her parents and to her Dubai-based 'would-be' boyfriend, and even Rupa too spoke to her sisters and uncle, at times, using that landline phone.

One Saturday afternoon when I was sitting at the kitchen nook and tasting a delicious chicken meal made by Rupa, a call rang out, aloud. Rashmi and Niyatidi both had gone to the nearby grocery store for buying household stuff. Rupa and I remained home. Rashmi had bought a two-wheeler, which used to come in handy and convenient for buying small items and quick fixes.

"Hello!" I rushed from the kitchen and picked up the call, panting slightly.

"Hey, all okay?" A familiar voice seeped through my ear.

"Hi! How did you get this number?" I had no idea how I remembered Shamik's voice.

"Not bad… listen, wanna meet?" His voice came sharp and slightly commanding to my ears.

"Umm…now?" I said hesitating.

"Yes… now!" He said, and I smiled inwardly.

"Ok…but where?" Shamik's face became so prominent in front of my eyes.

Why was he calling me, all of a sudden?

"At the bakery shop below Lifestyle?" He said, and I started calculating the time that might take for me to reach that place.

"I can be there in ten minutes!" My eyes toggled between the clock and my new red top that I took out for pressing just a couple of minutes ago.

"Good!" I could hear his smile from the other end, and it made me blush.

The next five minutes went busy putting on a dress and applying a mild makeup that highlighted my eyes and lips. I wore the red shirt and black jeans. My short hair looked messy, and I clicked a choker around my neck, giving me a tomboy look.

When I approached the bakery porch, I saw Shamik waiting in a reddish-brown shirt and black jeans. He smiled at me as I walked up the stairs to go closer to him. *Be careful of that boy*. My sister's words echoed in my brain. And a half-cheeked smile greeted him.

"Hey, looking good!" he smiled. "Let's have something in the bakery; I'm hungry!" He said, and I nodded with a smile. I followed him as he held the door for me. It felt good.

Our conversation was short but friendly and comfortable. We shared a pastry and two puffs and some coke. We hadn't spoken anything about girlfriends, boyfriends, or affairs. It was very general, and we were happy about our general talks.

After about half an hour, we got up to leave. But when we walked to the door and pushed it to exit, I saw Niyatidi and

Rashmi with Niyatidi's best friend Arko standing right in front of me. It suddenly freaked me out as she stared at me with wide eyes, and then her eyes went to Shamik. *It was as if she saw a ghost!*

"What are you guys doing here?" she asked, extremely curious. Her friend Arko made a strange face seeing Shamik with me.

"We just happened to bump into each other…" he tried to cover up our planned meeting.

Was he trying to save me or himself or both?

"But you were supposed to be home?" di said, and I gazed down. After a short group conversation, Shamik left, and I joined my sister and her friends. We went to the same bakery again. The person at the cash counter gave me a confused look.

"You know, he is having an affair with his senior, a girl from our batch!" Arko cracked the gossip while sipping his Pepsi.

"Stay away from him, Nihar, please!" Niyatidi sounded pushy and vexed.

I nodded blankly.

Abhik's visit to our house became a frequent thing over time. He used to tag along with his friend Arko each time whenever Arko came to teach computer lessons to my sister. Niyatidi had no interest in computers before Arko started helping her out on the same, but slowly her interest grew stronger both in computers and in Arko.

Rupa and I used to watch them study together, giggle, blush, chitchat. At times they used to pull the bedroom door almost to close, making our eyebrows raise. We eyed each other many times. Rupa always used to cough before entering the room, which would embarrass them.

On the other hand, Abhik mostly settled in our balcony playing guitar at times and at times, talking to Rupa. My mind often ran through the moments when Shamik and I met but didn't want to make out any meaning from it.

One day, during a casual discussion on socializing with boys, when Abhik asked me about the boys in my college, and I told him that my college is a women's college, then I noticed a strange happiness in his eyes. He did not try to hide it either, but I ignored and drifted the topic to a different direction. Because of my young age and introvert character, I often felt shy discussing love, romance, sex and other intimate stuff. Abhik's eyes used to trail me each time I walked past the balcony, and I could notice that very well. His often and 'no reason' visits to our house were giving me an indication that he was falling for me. Falling for Rupa was mostly not possible since Rupa had already made him her 'rakhi' brother.

Then came a day when Abhik wanted to convey his feelings to me. I knew that the day was approaching soon and spoke to Niyatidi about it, but she took it too casually and advised me not to pay much attention to his words.

One afternoon, being unaware of Abhik's presence in the house, I came out of the bathroom in a pink Turkish towel and tiptoed into the bedroom avoiding too much water dripping on the floor. Rupa shouted from the kitchen.

"I have just mopped the floor. Why don't you wipe yourself completely before exiting the bathroom?"

Sure, she had been already slogging since morning!

Rupa's last statement was faint, like a murmur, and I hardly paid any attention to it and proceeded to the room. Rupa trailed me and then started wiping the wet floor between the bathroom and the bedroom.

As I entered the room, a gent's cologne fragrance became prominent, and I got a shock of my life seeing Abhik sitting in front of our computer. He was engrossed watching a video. The door behind me closed with a click, and I stood almost frozen, cursing Rupa for not intimating me about his presence in the bedroom. The click sound broke his concentration, and he looked at me with darting eyes. Water was dripping all over starting from my head to toe; the towel was soaked and clung to my body like tree bark.

"Oh no!" the back of my throat choked mildly. I tried to cover myself more by crossing my arms in front of my chest. The towel was thin and wet. I could feel drops of water dripping from my hair to my chest, making their way to the towel.

"Shit!" He got up instantly. He was equally embarrassed, "Sorry, I'm leaving!" I moved from the door, and he made his way to the door but suddenly stopped. My heart skipped a beat. He looked over his shoulder. His eyes locked mine. My stomach churned, and heart thumped as he walked back to me. I moved further to the wall. He came closer, his arms locked me, and his nose inhaled my wet skin, without touching my skin, from the shoulder to my ear. My lips automatically opened as if I wanted to kiss him. I breathed hard, and he smiled. He placed a small peck near my ear, and I could feel the softness of his lips. Then he left the room abruptly, and I stood still for another couple of minutes trying to internalize what just happened.

Chapter 3

Tickets to Guwahati, our home town, had already been booked, but due to a delay in a project, Niyatidi's ticket had to be postponed, which made it obvious that I had to travel all by myself for two nights and three days to get to my city.

In the evening, our landline phone rang out loud, and louder was my mother's tone.

"How can you send Nihar alone? Let her stay with you!" Maa shouted at Niyatidi from the other side of the line.

"No Maa, I will have to leave for Bangalore for the project, and it would be really helpful if Rupa is with me. And there is no point for Nihar to wait for me! She can rather spend more time with you there! I'll be busy, and what will she do there for ten days?" My sister tried to justify her point. Rupa's eye kept toggling between Niyatidi and me as she was totally in the dark about the whole subject and trying to comprehend the matter from the context.

"But how would she come alone?" My mom's next question shot like a rocket. Her voice maintained the same tempo.

"Umm… let me try finding someone who can travel with her." Sister mumbled.

"Who? Boy?" My dad's curious intervention.

"I don't know, baba! But let me try finding someone, and I will call you by tonight!" Niyatidi, frustrated and tired after the whole day's practical exam plus the strict queries from parents.

She slumped down on our favorite orange bean bag with a sigh, exhaling a deep breath. "Rupa, water please!"

"Now what?" I asked, standing next to the door, thoughtful; my fingers ran through the wooden frame of the door.

"Are we going to Bangalore? Is it cold there?" the question came from Rupa's side while filling water from our plastic filter. From the side view, a gleam of excitement was prominent on Rupa's face.

"I think Shamik is traveling on the same day..." Niyatidi's statement came like a confused thought, and the name rang a bell in my head yet again.

Shamik!

Following week:

Niyatidi and Rupa both came to drop me off at the railway station. I had a haircut and got my eyebrows done the day before to look neater, probably a little show-off to my friends at my hometown.

We three met Shamik at a tea stall on platform number four. He looked good wearing the same reddish shirt that he wore during our bakery meet. With a broad charming smile on his face, he waited for us, clutching a moderately small travel bag in his hand. His eyes broadened for a fraction of a second seeing my new hairstyle, but I did not miss noticing his reaction. Niyatidi's face had lines of worry. She was still hesitant about the decision of sending me with Shamik. But we didn't have many options either.

"Hey!" He said as Di and Shamik exchanged a formal smile. Rupa maintained a straight face, and I felt a bit conscious experiencing their weird encounter. I knew that Niyatidi took that decision most unwillingly.

Even though Shamik and I hadn't met more than two times, a strange bonding of friendship existed between us. Everyone spoke to me about his compromised character and his womanizer side, but he never flaunted anything like that to me, and hence it was not possible for me to judge him that way. He was very friendly and helpful, and even in the way he looked at me, I never found a hint of anything strange or fishy.

We proceeded to our compartment, which was two compartments away from the rugged door of that second-class non/AC. One of the lower berths was assigned to me, and the middle to him. We dumped our luggage on the seat, and he started to put them away underneath the lower berth. I took my house slippers out of my bag, which was wrapped in a plastic cover, replacing them with my good shoes. Shamik was busy taking his Walkman and cassettes out of his backpack. Niyatidi rolled her eyes with a frown.

Show off!

She murmured.

Our eyes scanned through the compartment. Opposite to us, there was a newly married couple who looked happy and overwhelmed with each other's care and concern. A moderately old couple occupied the side berths, and one person who seemed to be traveling alone seemed drowsy. He continued to sleep sitting at one corner of the seat. I said bye to Niyatidi and Rupa, and Di hugged me tight. "Be good! No eyeliner, no lipstick, ok!" she whispered into my ears. "Come on, Di!" I eyeballed her and quickly checked if Shamik was hearing any of our conversations. He looked busy with his stuff, but we exchanged a quick gleam of a smile. I walked up to the door with Niyatidi and Rupa. They got down waving at me, and I walked back to my seat after bidding bye to them.

Shamik sat next to me plugging in his headphones.

"All okay? Are you comfy? Do you need anything?" He asked with a smile. His elbow slightly touched my arm.

"I am okay..." I nodded. A friendly smile got exchanged between us. I admired his smile. He nodded and became busy with his Walkman.

The train started after the signal shrilled high. Gentle breeze started to flow in, giving us some relief from the hot weather. As we were getting away from the busy platform, the noise started to fade away, and an eerie quietness started to take over the void air. People slowly settled in since it was going to be a long journey of two nights and three days.

I enjoyed the beautiful greenery outside the window and occasionally shared glances with Shamik, making sure that we are connected. Sipping water from the bottle that he bought for us, I looked at the setting sun, which looked gorgeously orange. Its beaming rays fell on the window rods and on our faces. Next time when I looked at Shamik, we exchanged a little longer gaze, as if his eyes noticed something on my face. The look lingered a while, making me a bit conscious. We smiled without knowing the reason. Our on and off short conversations went on in between his songs and my engrossed nature watch. They were mostly casual conversations, mostly about music. We shared a packet of biscuits. A random seller came into the compartment calling out, "coffee... coffee!" We had purchased coffee from him. The paper cups were so flimsy with wetness and heat from the coffee seeping through it. The coffee tasted like hot water with hardly any coffee powder in it.

My eyes looked around, checking out the compartment. Seeing me bored, he offered me one of his earplugs, and I took it immediately. I shoved it into my ear. We came closer than before, more friendly, more comfortable with each other.

At night, after dinner, I settled down next to the window once again. But then I had a magazine in my hand. I managed to purchase the magazine during a stop at a deserted station where we went down for a small walk and stretched our bodies over a small talk. My neck and back were hurting. I sighed, remembering that I left my pouch of medicines on the breakfast table itself.

My eyes looked up from the book when the couple opposite to us turned off their side lights, making the compartment dimmer. I flapped closed the book and tuned to see Shamik. He was trying to fix an air pillow for himself.

Why didn't I bring one?

I cursed myself staring at his pillow, and his eyes caught my look.

"You want?" He asked with a gesture of handing over the pillow to me.

I nodded in denial. "No, I don't mind sleeping without a pillow, used to it!" I covered up my pillow problem with a lie. I wasn't sure whether he believed it or not, but he shrugged his shoulders.

The old couple switched off their lights and dozed off to sleep soon. The lady got up after a while and passed a tablet to her husband and a bottle of water, and he swallowed it with a sip of water and returned the bottle to her and went back to sleep. Soon their snoring went prominent yet not very loud. The compartment was darker than before now. And the time was around 10.30 PM.

"Do you want to sleep?" Shamik asked me.

"Yes, in some time maybe. I'm not sleepy…" I said when he nodded. "Do you want to sleep?"

"It's ok… I'll sleep when you will sleep!" His answer was soothing to my ears.

When I looked around, I saw the couple sitting opposite to us got engrossed making out. When the husband tried to grab her here and there, she giggled, pushing hands away yet with a strong urge in her eyes. He fondled her hair, touched her neck, shoulders. She must have moaned, but I thanked God the sound got suppressed by the train's noise and occasional shrills. Their side was dark, but their activities were visible to us. I quietly turned off the light that was there on our side. My heart thumped, feeling nervous and uneasy.

"Hey... do you wanna sit near the door for some time?" Shamik elbowed. His elbowing gesture was pretty unusual but sweet.

I gave him a blank stare, and he pulled me along, clutching my hand, maneuvering through the silent aisle of the compartment. We settled near the door. Misty breeze percolated through my dupatta as I wrapped it around my neck. We sat silently next to each other, listening to songs from his Walkman. Without my knowledge, I dozed off and found myself leaning on his shoulder when I woke up.

"Shit! I'm so sorry!" I felt embarrassed finding myself sleeping on his shoulder. The wetness on my skin from my sweat and the heat on my ear could tell me that I had been sleeping for quite some time then.

I bit my tongue. Stared at him in embarrassment.

"It's alright! No worries!" his lips murmured. His face was hardly a couple of inches away from my face, and I could feel the warmth of his skin. The back of my throat choked, and a twinge of something clutched my heart. My sensory nerves wanted to linger the moment, and Shamik's eyes were searching for something deep into my eyes. I closed my eyes, and he closed his eyes, and then I turned to the other side sharply. It looked as though he was controlling himself from doing something, and so as I.

"Let's go back!" he got up slowly, and I followed him back to our place.

Next day, I woke up with a bad headache. It was hotter than other days as we were crossing the dry deserted lands of

Andhra Pradesh. Sandy, no trace of water, and a hot dry air made everyone restless.

More natural foods like cucumber with salt and red pepper, coconut water, and dates were getting sold inside the train. Kids relished cold drinks and ice creams, and the train started to get noisier as people began to interact and make new friends. I clutched my eye as my migraine hammered my head non-stop. When I told him about my migraine, Shamik asked me to rest my head on a pillow on his lap, and I did the same. He stroked my hair slowly, and that delivered quite a relaxation to me. I rested well for some time, and he kept holding my forehead every now and then. The old couple gave us a weird stare, and that embarrassed me. A smile of mischief brushed his lips, and I got up.

"What happened?" he asked, the smile still lingering on his lips.

"Nothing! I feel better now…" I adjusted my hair, which was still messy. I settled with a bottle of water, looking at the horizon.

My eyes drifted at him, and he smiled again.

"Why are you smiling?" I asked without thinking much.

"Why? Isn't smiling good for health?" his eyes scanned through my eyes.

"Yes… of course!" I said and looked outside the window, and he became busy talking to the man opposite to him. I was not interested in the conversations.

That night, I decided to sleep early because I wanted to skip the late-night romance of the neighboring couple, and

Shamik did understand that. I just gave an excuse for being sleepy. He knew that it was the previous night's scene that I wanted to avoid.

But things looked different that night. It looked like that night the couple refused to even talk to each other. And they slept quietly, earlier than us and refrained from talking to each other.

I lied down on the lower berth, double folding the bedsheet and shoving it under my head, and Shamik was already lying down on the middle berth.

"Looks like there was a fight!" he announced, but he spoke in our mother tongue so that people don't understand.

"Possible!" I replied, smiling internally.

"Were they the reason you wanted to sleep early?" he kept dragging the topic.

I didn't reply.

"Are you sleeping?" his fingers ran through the side of my berth. They didn't touch me though.

"No…you?"

"No," he replied. There was a book in his hand with which he rubbed my left arm lightly.

"Isn't it too dark for reading a book?" I asked.

"Hmm… tomorrow I will show you a trick." He said, now his face peeped down.

"What trick?" I asked. My eyes wide open. I adjusted my bedsheet.

"God! I'm not looking at anything." He said promptly, and I felt embarrassed. He didn't miss to notice it.

"What trick?" I repeated my question.

"A trick to find your soulmate!" He said looking at me.

"Wow! How?" My answer and the question had a hint of smirk mixed in it.

"Tomorrow..." he curled in his hand and went back to his original position. I dozed off in sometime.

Two nights were over, and it was not as bad as I thought it would be. On the contrary, the journey felt safe and comfortable. I felt as if I was traveling with a long-known friend of mine with whom I could share my problems, with whom I could share most kinds of talks. Our bonding of friendship became stronger with the train journey. I found a good friend in Shamik.

The next day, he showed me the trick. It was a trick of finding the first letter of one's soulmate's name by reading the crisscrossed lines on his or her thumb.

"Let me show you the thing!" He took my hand, but I curled it back promptly. "Hey, do you feel awkward so frequently?" he grabbed my hand in a friendly yet forceful way, and I pursed my lips. He started to look into the lines. I stared at him.

"Can you read a letter there?" He asked me.

"No..." I tried looking deep, concentrating, trying to figure any letter there but didn't find any. At times I saw an 'H' there, and other times I saw 'K' there, but just didn't say anything.

"I think you have 'S' in those lines." He said.

"Really?" We shared a glance. Gentle breeze played with my hair when he moved a single hair that bothered my right eye. Our eyes locked for a couple of seconds making my heart beat high. "Someone whose name starts with 'S'!" He further added.

S?...Is he flirting?

I smiled, shook my head. Even his name started with 'S'. I thought internally but pretended not to remember that.

I wanted to ask what his finger said but refrained myself from asking fearing what if he said 'N'.

I curled my arms in and then looked out. I calculated the number of hours left to reach our destination.

We reached our station, and he helped me pack my baggage. I looked at the compartment one last time to refresh the memories that we created in these two nights and three days. My cousin brother was already waiting at the platform to receive me, and hence, a long conversation didn't happen between Shamik and me. A crisp bye and a glance made us realize that we were going to miss the time that we had spent on the train. We bade bye to each other, and our ways parted like how it just parted when we met Niyatidi at the entrance of the bakery.

Chapter 4

Two months later:

Niyatidi breezed in through the open door of our living room. Her ponytail bounced on her shoulder in a funny gait. She pushed the door to close with a slight touch of her hip and then dropped her belongings carelessly on the already overloaded table next to the door.

I lay down on the divan leaning against the wall with a pillow between my arms. I felt a bit feverish, and a boil above my eye irritated me as I tried to pry that out.

"All ok? You look reddish!" Niyatidi touched my forehead and felt my raised temperature, lines of worry on her forehead. "Show me your tongue," her command echoed. I giggled with a pale face. "Rupa! Our doctor is here!"

Rupa's loud laugh rang in our small kitchen space.

"Shut up!" Niyatidi.

"How can I shut up and still show my tongue?" I annoyed her more.

Rupa came and stood leaning on the corridor beam between the kitchen and the hall. A smile suppressed her lips.

"Nihar di is not well since morning. Her mouth feels tasteless, and she also has a fever and body ache," Rupa announced and paused. "She has some boils on her face and one on the chest..." Her last sentence triggered more worry on Niyatidi's face.

"Damn! It's a season for Chicken pox!" Niyatidi sat down next to me as Rupa handed her a glass of water.

"Chicken pox!" we cried out in chorus.

The boil above my eye broke out, releasing some watery kind of liquid.

"Don't touch it!" Rupa screamed.

"Let's go to a doctor, Nihar!" Niyatidi said, and I nodded. "Thank God Rashmi went to her hometown. This is pretty contagious." I felt some sense of relief in Niyatidi's voice.

We went to see a doctor near our house, and he confirmed that I had chicken pox and hence I must stay home until the boils dry up. My mother's phone call gave us all kinds of instructions. They were mainly for Rupa. Rupa did follow them well. I felt very weak for about ten days with more boils breaking out on various parts of my body. They all contained water and felt extremely itchy. Rupa used to pluck fresh neem leaves from one of our neighbor's houses and wash them and lay them underneath my bed. She used to grind fresh turmeric roots and then mix them with neem paste and apply on my body and face and then sponge my skin lightly with a soft cloth. I was confined to one room and stayed away from Niyatidi and Rupa. Only white pumpkin soup with mashed rice was given to me for eating for ten days. My mouth felt no taste, and my head always heavy with an ache. My only work was reading books, or listening to music, or watching repetitions of the same movie laying or sitting on my bed and be in my room.

One of those days, Niyatidi walked into my room and sat next to me maintaining a little distance. She too started getting the same symptoms.

"Did Abhik talk to you regarding anything?" She asked, her eyes looked pale like how it was for me initially.

"No…why? And regarding what?" I asked; my mind ran through the memory of that day when Abhik came closer than usual. But Niyatidi wasn't aware of that incident as I feared to share that with her or Rupa. My throat suddenly felt lumpy, and I downed it with a swallow.

Does she know about it already? My mind voice echoed.

"No, he didn't!" My answer was neat and free of any confusion.

"He said he loves you! And it seemed like you are interested as well. Is that true?" Niyatidi curled in her legs into the small red chair and settled in. Rupa came with a mug full of boiled bitter guard juice for me and a cup of tea for Niyatidi.

"I've never told him that I am interested! Yes, I could feel that he has feelings toward me, but I haven't reciprocated anything similar to him!" My mind ran through the after-bath intimacy again and thought if I could have done a better job by stopping him that day. Because I didn't show an objection, and he took that as 'yes', and hence the confusion arose.

"So Can I tell him that you aren't interested?"

Didi asked, and I nodded. "What about Arko and you? Is everything alright between you two?" I sipped my juice. Rupa made a brush with neem leaves which came handy for skin irritation.

Niyatidi frowned. "Nope! We called it off!"

"You never told anything about it!" again, a chorus from Rupa and me.

Di remained quiet, and her silence implied that she didn't want to talk more about that. So we kept quiet as well.

"Did anything happen between you and Abhik…umm… like" Niyatidi paused, which rose suspicion in my mind.

"Like what?" I asked anxiously.

"Like… did you guys kiss or maybe more?" Her eyes narrowed.

"No!" I felt embarrassed. Rupa moved a little away toward the wall. Dramatic! Her eyes were fixed on me.

"Hmm…"

A frail knock on the main door startled all of us. Rupa rushed to the sound, and Niyatidi followed her. I downed the juice and then curled in underneath the blanket with a book in hand.

"What a surprise!" Niyadi's voice came through the chink in the door.

Shamik.

After our train journey, we never got a chance to meet each other.

Too many gossips swarmed around him, and hence I wanted to stay away.

I exhaled a sigh!

Shamik entered with a small bouquet of flowers. His perfume felt familiar to me, reminding me of our train journey. I looked at him with a formal smile.

His black shirt and light blue jeans looked good on him. His clean-shaved face and after-bath look made him look very handsome. Niyatidi, after a brief talk with him, left the room. But I could see her seated in the living room through the ajar bedroom door. Rupa walked out of the kitchen with a bag in her hand and went out to get some produce for dinner. The sole of her slippers grated the corridor floor, reminding me of my pet peeve.

"For you!" Shamik handed me the flowers and settled on the chair next to my bed where di was sitting just a minute ago.

"Thank you!" I took the flowers from him and looked around to find a place for the flowers.

"Let me help you..." he took them from me and placed them next to my desktop computer and walked back to the chair. My eyes saw him walking across the room and trailed him back once he was seated.

"If you don't know chicken pox is pretty contagious, and you shouldn't have come over." I said playing with a stray thread from my thick blanket. I adjusted it further up covering up till my neck.

"I don't care about many things in life. I do what my heart says to do!" his sharp answer yet again churned my core.

"Btw, why are you shoving yourself under the blanket? Come on! I'm not gonna attack you or something!" his comment threw me into a fit of giggle.

We spent the rest of the evening, almost until 8.30 PM, just by talking and smiling. Niyatidi took a nap, and Rupa finished most of the works in the kitchen. She gave a mug of coffee and biscuits to him in between our chitchat. When leaving, Shamik touched my cheek in a very mild stroke. "Get well soon!" his touch was soft but it gave me an urge, as if I wanted him to linger his fingers on my cheek for some more time. Our eyes locked for a moment, and then he left quickly after bidding bye to Niyatidi and Rupa.

Shamik's face, our conversations, kept blocking my memory stacks every now and then for a long time.

That was the last time we met during our college days. I kept hearing about him from Niyatidi, but every time it was in connection to some kind of female character, and hence my thoughts faded further away and eventually I totally stopped thinking about him.

When Niyatidi's marriage got fixed, we all moved to a house next to her in-laws', which was about six to seven kilometers north of our old house. Contact with Abhik faded away like the diminishing smoke in the air, and we were busy in di's marriage.

A couple of days before di's wedding, one day I saw Abhik, seated in the same bus, on the way to my college. He gave me a stranger look, and I too avoided talking to him. His feelings for me might have been genuine, but it couldn't break through my soul. His friend Arko stopped talking to Niyatidi, and Abhik stopped talking to me. We all moved on.

Niyatidi moved to the United States right after her wedding. I waited for my turn, and after a year and a half, even I moved there as well. Our parents kept shuttling between India and the US initially, but eventually, they got bored, tired, and planned to stay in India. Once a year, we visited them and stayed with them for about one month. They were growing old.

During one of my visits to India, I happened to bump into Shamik. It was a serendipitous encounter, and we both were amazed seeing each other. We were more refined physically, mentally, and psychologically, but still, the same vibe persisted between us, the same vibe we shared when our paths collided each time.

It was a sultry summer evening. The warmth of the setting sun seeped through the dry sand on the shore. I was casually sitting a few inches away from the water with my close friend Riyaz. Riyaz was not my boyfriend, but we shared a relationship that was a little more than just friends. We had a romantic encounter while dancing in a pub during our reunion party with friends, and since then he started liking me. It happened in a local pub. While dancing when we came closer, closer than usual, he ran his fingers through my arms looking into my eyes. An instant urge of making love grew stronger in both of us. But the place being a public place, we kept it limited to a passionate lip-lock. His fingers yet worked though the bare back of mine as we moved to a dark nook avoiding my friends' eyeshot. Our raised hormones made our blood rush as I felt him raising hard against my skin. I could hardly control getting an orgasm, but after a couple of minutes, we came back to the dance floor when my best friend Dina eyeballed me. I was physically attracted to him. We used to love each other's company. Drinking wine with him used to take things to a different level.

That day, when I was sitting with Riyaz clutching his hand, a familiar face flashed in front of my eyes. I blinked my eyes a couple of times to see if he was the same person whom I thought he would be. And fortunately or unfortunately, he was it. It was Shamik. He looked different, sharper, more intelligent, casually dressed up. He had put on weight and looked like a man than a college-goer. There was a flamboyant aura around him, and I could feel that. My soul processed a smile in my core. He was accompanied by one of his friends and seemed busy in some discussion with him.

"Hey, look at you!" he stopped right in front of me making me blush. His shoes gleamed bright and looked pricey. An instant happiness brushed through my heart seeing him after five years. My hair grew longer then, and I looked more like a woman, ditching my tomboyish look. I wore a red salwar with loaded kajal rimming my eyes and a pair of dangling earrings. My hair went about my face, and his eyes looked at me strangely.

"Hey…how are you? Oh my God!" we shook hands lingering the hands more into a clutch. I giggled. I caught a twinkle of excitement in his eyes.

"I am good! And you look so different!" I admired his new look. Probably even he was admiring me, my gut said.

"Do I?" He blushed. We stared at each other for a minute as the silence took over making the air fill with awkwardness. We fell lack of words letting only a void take over.

I gently pulled away my hand, and he too looked over his shoulder and signaled his friend to wait for a minute. His friend walked alone and settled next to a peanut seller.

Finally, Shamik broke the conversation.

"So boyfriend?" He asked, eyeing at Riyaz.

I blushed, "kind of!"

"My kind of or your kind of?" Shamik's quirky question threw me into a giggle yet again.

"Your kind of!"

"Hmm… interesting! Well… carry on!" He said. Riyaz got a bit restless noticing our eyes on him.

"Really nice to see you!" He stepped back. I felt a strange heaviness on my chest seeing him leave.

"You take care!"

He walked away and joined his friend. I stood there frozen for a moment as he looked back at me briefly. We both smiled. It was a smile of recognition, friendship, and promise between two souls. He vanished into the throngs of people at the seashore.

Time flew by once again, making us go away from each other, making us settle into our own lives with our own duties and responsibilities.

Chapter 5

20 years later:
Seattle, USA

We drove past the Redmond town center, our once upon a time hangout place. The closely packed shops bore authentic flavors of variety fudges and pretzels. Small boutiques had eye-catching cotton and linen outfits. Glass and beads jewelries dazzled in both vivid and subtle colors. The nearby farmer's market seemed closed for the day. The neighboring children's park looked a little deserted compared to other weekends. The sky started to get duskier, and Vinod pulled over the car to the curbside near Tiffany's showroom. Our house was hardly a mile away from Redmond center, but we planned to settle down in the park for a few breaths of fresh air before going back into the confines of the house.

"Will you be okay to walk?" Vinod said, extending his hand to me for support.

"Come on! I'm not pregnant." My lopsided smile portrayed my irked mood. Few shots of methotrexoide on my butt to get rid of my ectopic pregnancy made me exhausted yet again, both physically and mentally. My face was sullen, but then, I tried to tone down myself.

"I'm fine, don't worry..." I moved his hand gently from my shoulder and got out of the car. His hand felt heavy, and I was feeling weak.

We sat on one of the benches placed next to the small fountain at the corner of the park. Vinod, my husband, sat next to me, clutching my hand. His warm rub on my fingers smoothened a part of the hollowness of my mind as I exhaled a sigh. The moss-fringed green fence around us delivered a calming fragrance and a serene view.

"Why don't you take a trip to India and be with Maa for a month?" he looked at me with compassion, but we ended up sharing an empty glance that lingered for a couple of seconds.

Niyatidi's sister-in-law's son's upanayanam (holy thread) function is also happening early next month, and they had invited us multiple times.

Thoughts ran in my mind. A sudden urge to visit India came in those thoughts. The monotonous life abroad and prolonged try of conceiving was draining me out completely.

Is life all about getting pregnant?

My mind echoed.

"Let me book your tickets to India! What's say?" He demanded an assertive answer. I nodded. "And you?"

"I can't… right now, but please take your mind off of this pregnancy, this IVF… miscarriage! If nothing is working out, we will adopt a child!" Vinod urged, looking into my eyes. It churned my core. A drop of tear rolled down my right eye and landed on my maroon short-sleeved frock, wetting it like a dot. The street lights shone bright by then.

Ten years of our marriage had gone by, and we were childless. It bothered us, and more than us, it bothered our parents. But recently more than being childless, going through all the medical procedure to make an IVF pregnancy successful frustrated me. I just wanted to run away from the life that I was leading. Even though professionally I was an engineer, validating requirements for software projects, I was a writer by passion. My husband stood by me prioritizing my health, but within his inner self, he was craving to become a father, and I could just feel it every moment from every conversation he cracked.

We shared a soft kiss. I closed my eyes feeling the warmth of his palm on my chin.

My stomach had a mild churn with an ache.

“Btw how’s your next book coming along?” Vinod tried to bring up a normal conversation. The orange sky looked vibrant, and a few small kids skating in the park looked extremely adorable.

“Good, I guess! Working on a thriller this time.” I said, knowing that Vinod was hardly interested in my stories.

“Interesting!” His raised eyebrow with a mischievous smile made me blush. “I’m not the villain there right?”

We broke into laughter. “Ok, let’s get going; I have a meeting scheduled at 9 PM and need to sort a few things before I get on the call.” He got up, stretching his arms in the air.

“Do you wanna pick up some quick bites from the supermarket? Or we can have dosa and leftover sambar from last night.” I said. Slowly getting up and walking to the car.

"I would prefer the latter." He opened the car door for me, and I slid slowly into the passenger seat next to the driver seat.

At night, when booking tickets, I sat next to Vinod. I grabbed the remote and started our usual sitcom on TV. My phone flashed a message notification. I opened it, and for a minute, I kept looking into the message.

It was a message from Shamik. I took the phone and walked to the open kitchen, reading the content of it.

"Hey, hope you are doing awesome! Any plans to visit India?" It was not like we had never messaged each other. Once in a blue moon, we did message on messenger but even then it became very rare and slowly stopped. I exhaled a deep breath.

"Hi, I am doing great! Thanks for asking. Hope everything is fine at your end too!" I typed and placed the phone next to the oven and started working on some veggies for the salad. The leftover dosa and sambhar didn't look to be sufficient for two. I opened the air fryer and shoved in a couple of seasoned fish fillets. I tossed the veggies and leaves in a red salad bowl with raspberry vinaigrette, salt, and white pepper. I stacked two plates and two bowls for fish and veggies at the coffee table while continuing to chat with Shamik.

"Nihar, why don't you keep the phone away for some time? Let's eat, honey, I'm starving!" Vinod came from behind to help me with the glasses. My fingers instantly went for the power button of the phone and kept it beside the fruit bowl on the kitchen aisle.

My Visit to India:

I enjoyed the vacation at my mother's place, away from my complicated and stressful life. Eating my favorite food cooked by dear mother with her unconditional love and care smoothed my mental and physical pain.

On Sundays, we used to visit our aunt at our old ancestral home, but that Sunday was different. We stayed home. I wanted to take a break as even in aunt's house few stereotyped minds haunted me every now and then deliberately discussing topics on pregnancy. In the evening, when I shuffled through a bunch of old photo albums sitting on our rustic wooden chair at the nook of our veranda, mom joined me with coffee and a jar full of biscuits.

"Why don't you ask Vinod to fly down… maybe sometime next week? I mean… if you are really serious about adopting a child!" The shrilling noise that she always made when sipping tea irked me and so as the topic.

"Please don't make that sound when having tea Maa…" I said annoyed, eyebrows furrowed, sticking my eyes to an old photo of my father where he looked very dapper in his favorite gray silk suit.

"I know, even your father used to hate that sound!" she became nostalgic while talking about Baba. Her next sip had the same noise but more controlled.

My father passed away thirteen years back from a massive heart attack in that small town where hospital facility was very minimal. Hospitals were hardly equipped with any advanced machines or technologies. To be honest there was hardly any hospital in that town. We lost our father and Maa lost her husband to that cardiac arrest all of a sudden at a young age. She started to live on her own, moved from the old house where we were born and brought up. My father's memories, especially a few details the day when he left us forever, kept haunting her every now and then, and hence she decided to move from our old house. We had always seen our mother's strong side. She always kept the weaknesses to herself.

"Maa! I feel like having coconut laddoo! Are you planning to make it this time?" I said stacking up the albums at one corner of the bamboo table.

"I can, if you eat… you remember last time you left the whole jar here, and then I had to finish it all!" she slowly got up from the chair and handed the mugs to Rupa. After both Niyatidi's and my marriage, Rupa moved back here, with Maa, helping her with daily chores. They both walked toward the kitchen and I turned on the backlight of my phone checking if Vinod had messaged. A few mosquitoes buzzing around my ears instigated me to close the windows.

There was no message from Vinod, but I saw a couple of messages in the notification bar. They were from Shamik.

"Can we meet up while you are in Chennai… of course if that's okay with you?" his message gave an instant smile on my face.

"Can I make some laddoo for your in-laws as well?" Mom's question from the kitchen brought a lopsided smile on my face. I stopped typing the reply and dropped the phone on the sofa, mind went blank as I took the remote to turn on the music player.

I looked at the phone blankly again.

"How about 2nd of July?" I typed, finally.

"Sure! I'll be there!" his reply came almost immediately after my message as if he was waiting for my response.

His images came strongly as I shuffled through my memory stack. I pulled the screen from our dressing table mirror and stood in front of it. I circled the rim of my eyes with a kohl pencil, making them noir.

"Nihardi, Maa is calling you to watch 'Srimoyi' (my mother's favorite television series)," Rupa intervened. Her talk unnerved me. I kept the eye pencil back in its usual place, pressed the pause button to stop the music player, and followed her to join my mother in her favorite serial.

My nephew's Upanayanam function was on July 1st, and Maa and I attended it along with my sister and her family. A series of rituals took place in a grand way before adorning the boy with the holy thread. It was a long day, and we all were exhausted by the time we came back to the hotel. Niyatidi preferred to stay in the hotel with us, ditching her in-law's house. My mind was restless thinking about my meeting with Shamik. I would be seeing him after almost two decades. I shuffled through the cupboard but didn't find any good dress.

But why am I trying to look beautiful?

My conscience made me guilty, and I decided to keep it simple. A black kurta with regular pair of jeans, my fingers brushed through the fabric. I removed all the heavy jewelry except the oxidized nose stud. I was very fond of it. I looked into the mirror, taking a dollop of night cream on my palm. My skin looked paler than how it used to look before. I was nearing forty years, and my skin had the impression of my age. I don't look as good as I used to during my college days. That thought made me conscious all of a sudden. I rubbed a mild shade of lipstick on my lips when Niyatidi noticed me.

"What's happening? Are you having a date?" Her sarcastic smile gave me a frown.

"What?" I rubbed the lipstick off with the towel that was perched on the headboard, embarrassed.

"Did Vinod call up?" she said coming closer, indirectly wanting to know if all was okay between Vinod and I.

"I'm fine di, feeling a bit tired. That's all." I totally skipped talking about Shamik's matter, refrained from telling her that I would be meeting him the very next day.

"What are you doing tomorrow? Are you joining us for the temple visit?"

"No, di. I want to take the day easy; moreover, I might visit one of my friends in the evening." I said as she gave me a disappointed look. "Okay…" She sighed and stepped into the bathroom, closing the door on her way in a squeaking noise.

"Hey, shall I send my in-laws' driver Raja Anna? He can be with you tomorrow for the rest of the day. Just make sure to send him back around 8 pm so that he can pick us up from Aunt's house." Niyatidi said peeping out of the ajar bathroom door.

"Not a bad idea! But can you please finish your shower first?" I walked to the mirror with a dab of under-eye cream between my fingers. "Hmm…" she finally closed the door.

Next day:

The morning sunlight had the usual heat and a succumbed humid in it. I perched the shades on the bridge of my nose on the way out from the hotel. The driver came out to check if I had any huge luggage with me. He flaunted a familiar smile, and I acknowledged it. I was on the way to meet Shamik at the Chamiers Café in RA Puram, Chennai. I dressed myself in a black kurta and faded blue jeans and wore a pair of acrylic black stud earrings. I left the last night's nose ring as is, which gave me a different look, a fusion of ethnic and trendy. My hair was short and highlighted with blueish silver streaks in between my black hair. The tufts of my hair felt a little rougher than how it used to feel in Seattle's weather. Change of water always took a toll on my hair. A series of bracelets mixed with a few bangles jingled on my left wrist, layering my tattoo, and I had my blue Movado watch on my right wrist.

Raja Anna, or the driver to be precise, knew most of the places in Chennai and hence it was pretty easy to find the café even without the help of any GPS. After about forty-five minutes on the road, we reached The Chamiers. Shamik called me once in between to let me know that he had already reached and had been waiting for me.

I got off the car and asked the driver to wait at the parking spot. He nodded with a smile. I handed him two hundred bucks for breakfast, and he grinned with extreme happiness.

"Don't worry, Madam. Just give me a call once you want to leave from here." He shared his phone number with me. His gesture of crossing his arms on his chest looked more like a habit to me. I smiled and nodded. I slowly climbed up the stairs, looking around and appreciating the interior of the café. A combination of antique and modern furniture made a contemporary fusion, and a store at the corner of the first floor displaying antique jewelry gave a high-end look to the café. The rusted finish on gold and silver attracted me to visit the store, but I was already running late. *Maybe next time,* my inner voice said. A combination of light blue and white interior was absolutely soothing for the eyes. As I entered the sitting area, an aroma of authentic filter coffee allured my senses. Shamik was sitting at the corner table next to the door that led to a balcony. He looked charmingly handsome in a white shirt and blue jeans. A pair of shades was on the bridge of his nose, an unlit cigarette poised between his fingers, and he looked occupied looking into his phone. I understood the reason behind choosing a table next to the balcony.

"Hey...!" I appeared right in front of him. My heart thumped rapidly, and I was not sure of the reason, but I tried hard to keep that to myself. We were meeting after decades, and I was excited and drawing a blank at the same time.

He got up from his chair and hugged me. His touch was warm... gentle. I could feel a familiar fragrance, I could feel the same warmth. "Hey... how are you? You look good!" he said, smiling. He looked handsome, matured. A hint of blush was there in his smile.

"You are looking handsome too!" I sat, admiring his salt and pepper hair color. Our age had taken over our looks.

Like me, even he was growing old, but it was graceful. He looked more attractive than before, maintaining the same mischievous smile on his face.

We spoke to each other as lingering glances got exchanged frequently during our conversations. His eyes were trying to read my eyes. And I could feel it. We had three rounds of filter coffee and a few toasts, some veggies and tuna salad. His smoking habit seemed to have increased as he grabbed his pack of fag and walked to the balcony, ushering me if I wanted to join. I followed him. I smoked a cigarette after a very long time. It gave me a strange happiness and relaxation. We sat on the staircase of the old building and spoke for a very long time. He shared his part of stories, and I did mine. Our lives sounded different than how it used to be during college days, complicated. We both grew matured. He had a wife and a daughter, he was well-settled in life. I had a husband and was trying to adopt a child after multiple failed pregnancies.

I looked around to check the surroundings. A few coconut trees fenced the place and rendered a healing touch to it. He suddenly held my hand, interlacing my fingers between his warm fingers, and I hesitated a little but didn't show it and let his palm clutch mine, switching the cigarette to the other hand.

"Nihar, are you happy?" he asked.

I nodded in assertion, smiling. "And what about you?"

He smiled, did not say anything.

It was thirty minutes past noon. He settled the bill, and we walked out of the café and got into the car. Raja Anna reversed the car with a grating noise, blowing a bulk of sand. I closed my eyes. Finally, we merged into the main road.

The next destination was the hotel where Shamik had booked his accommodation. He checked in, and we entered his room. Initially, I wanted to stay in the lobby, but then that might give him an odd feeling. Hence I decided to go with him. I craved for coffee again. My addiction for coffee was at the peak, and the side effect insomnia came like an advantage to me. I became a poet as a result of sleep deprivation. Shamik ordered two mugs of coffee and dal roti and chicken for lunch. When he went to freshen up, I lay down on the bed, exhausted. An aroma of soap trailed from the bathroom as I played a playlist of songs on my phone. I closed my eyes in relaxation. The bed felt comfortable, and I almost dozed off while listening to the soothing music. The waiter came with coffee and lunch, and I had to get up from the bed. I ushered him in, and at the same time, Shamik came out of the bath wearing yet another white attire. He looked and smelled fresh.

After settling the check, the waiter walked out, and I settled down on the couch with a mug of coffee. He played his favorite songs on his phone, and I wondered how he knew about all my favorite songs.

"I feel exhausted!" I murmured.

"Do you want a foot massage? Don't worry, I'm not a foot fetish!" He smiled, and I giggled.

"Why don't you take a nap?" he suggested, leaning back in the chair.

I moved to the bed, but the sleep was suddenly gone. Suddenly, I was feeling awkward. When I looked at him, I saw him looking back at me. Our eyes locked for the next couple of seconds, as if both of us were either in refusal to look away from each other or too tired to change the gaze. My stomach churned as I felt a twinge of something in my heart. Was that moment trying to deliver some kind of meaning to us? I wondered and then covered that with a giggle. His lips cracked into a witty smile.

"Hey, let's eat!" he ushered me to join him. I almost scrambled along the headboard and sat on the chair next to him. The old friendship was almost back, and I felt considerably comfortable with Shamik.

We ate while talking about the reminiscences of our college lives. Those are the stories that we would have shared if we had met during college time. Post-lunch, we decided to visit the beach where we had accidentally bumped into each other a couple of years ago. But I dozed off for a while without knowing what Shamik was doing. When he woke me up, it was about dusk.

"I know you are a deep sleeper, but I didn't know you snore!" He touched my hand with the back of his hand, and that skipped a breath from me. I bit my lips. "Sorry!"

"That's alright!" He switched on the night lamp for more brightness, and I walked to the bathroom to wash my face. We decided to visit the sea beach.

Our visit to the beach was as smooth as the shore breeze. We walked along the shore. At times, my hand brushed against his hand briefly, feeling the warmth of his skin. We settled at one of the small cafes next to the seashore. A few rounds of momos and cold coffees treated us as we experienced a cozy breezy evening. We captured ourselves in a selfie so that it could keep reminding us of that beautiful day.

Shamik hugged me tight. We were destined to part ways again. This time the hug was tighter, with more compassion, more warmth, and more emotions. Raja Anna looked a bit confused, and I was a bit hesitant even though I craved to linger in the hug. My eyes were moist, but I hid that feeling of mine under the darkness of the evening.

Shamik left, and I too left India after a week. My Seattle flight was waiting to take me back to my usual monotonous life.

Chapter 6

My trip back to Seattle was full of Shamik's thoughts. Even though we shared only friendly intimacy and nothing beyond that, his presence in my mind was unavoidable to my conscience.

Vinod received me at the Seattle airport. It was pretty hot and humid, unlike Seattle's usual. We took the highway 5, followed by taking an exit and then merged onto the broad road of Bellevue and then reached Redmond city after driving for about fifty minutes. The mild drizzle with floating pollen in it was soothing to me. Vinod got irked though and adjusted his shades as he was allergic to the pollen.

A hot shower was soothing, and a mug of hot coffee with my usual biscuits were just about perfect with it. I slept away the day on our living room couch, and Vinod sat next to me doing his office works, enjoying his favorite sitcom on TV simultaneously. By evening, I felt fresher. I walked to the kitchen and cut veggies and chicken for a stew and toasted some sourdough bread with extra butter. Vinod relished that meal, and I could just sense it. He might have been bored of taking the quick fixes. I fixed him a bowl of marshmallow cereal as he craved for something sweet, and then we walked into our bedroom.

The soft bed felt softer as my body sank into the plushness of it. Vinod switched off the lights and joined me in bed, almost awaking me up from a drowsy head. He kissed my forehead and caressed my hair that flew about my face and neck. My fingers reached to the switchboard to stop the fan from oscillating. His kisses felt tender, and I inhaled deep, acknowledging his warmth. His fingers traveled through my skin, making their way to the high of my chest. I smirked. "What are you up to?"

"Let's make love!" his lips touched my lobes, whispering the words into my ear. From the lobes, fringing my neckline, he stopped where the neckline of my night dress started. His moist breathing felt inviting on my skin. I lifted my hands, and he pulled my satin one-piece nighty effortlessly and dropped that on the floor. All I was left with on my body was the white panty. I felt myself aroused, slightly wet between my legs already. He cupped my breast in passion, and I moaned at the back of my throat. I felt him hard against me. We got rid of the blanket as it started getting unusually hot. I arched myself to take him in. We occasionally smooched in that process of making love. Shamik's face came prominent in front of me every now and then; the time we spent in the hotel, the way he looked at me, the way his hand brushed against mine, his warm lingering hug, everything. I clutched my eyes sharply to get rid of his thoughts. My body still rhythmically moved with Vinod. Due to the dim light, he couldn't figure much of my lost expressions. We fell exhausted after the lovemaking session, and Vinod dozed off to sleep quickly after that. Shamik kept hovering my thoughts for the rest of the night.

Six months later:

The decision of our temporary relocation to Delhi was taken suddenly, and within a month or two, we moved to Delhi.

The main reason behind it was pursuing adoption that we had been thinking of for quite some time. For Vinod, it was not that difficult as his office had a branch in Delhi, and his role of a global manager justified the feasibilities of spending a couple of years in India. We had vacated our house in Seattle and dumped all the belongings into a U-Haul storage, which we rented for the following three years. Both my body and soul were way too exhausted from all the apparent IVF treatments, and hence we had to come up with that alternate way to fill the emptiness of our lives by adopting a child.

After moving to India, thoughts about Shamik started to get stronger in my brain. My conscience kept pushing his thoughts away, but they kept returning like the ocean waves… stronger, louder, crushing into my thoughtful mind. The frequency of Shamik's calls ramped up too. Initially, I started avoiding his calls, but at times, I felt bad for ignoring him. Vinod and I rented a fully furnished house in Delhi. But we had to visit Chennai frequently to complete the adoption formalities. Vinod's usual office work started. I had two maids working for me, one was taking care of cooking, and her daughter was taking care of the rest of the household chores. I decided to concentrate on writing the next script for my next project.

One day, a call on my messenger surprised me, or I could say shocked me. It was a call from Abhik. He had always been there as a social media friend, but we hardly interacted. He became a filmmaker and was working on corporate ad films or documentaries made for NGOs. After a brief conversation over messenger, he said that he would wish to brainstorm on a couple of topics on his upcoming films. I invited him home one day over a cup of coffee. We discussed many things and found ourselves more matured and old enough to surpass those silly feelings of our college times. He showed me his pencil drawings, and I admired them. I found deep meanings in all his artworks. The funky wildness of his behavior had toned down a lot. He told me about his ideas of publishing a book on pictorial poems. We shared quality time, and then when Vinod came home from the office, he joined us as well. I felt good after seeing Abhik after a very long time.

Literature Fest in Odisha:

The Odisha literature festival was around the corner. I was preparing to showcase my just-published romantic fiction on their literary platform. The event organizers agreed to launch my novel on the first day of the event, and I was assigned a span of ten minutes to talk about my book, my background, and my passion for art and literature. Vinod had always been supportive of me even though he was never interested in reading my books or knowing the subject I was writing about. But he was generous enough to invest his time to book my tickets. I spoke to one of the organizers over the telephone, and he informed us that a double-bedroom had been assigned and allocated for my stay over there. I was trying to coax Vinod into the trip since it would be my first literature fest in India, and I was a bit hesitant to visit there all by myself.

"Hey, please join me! Feels pretty weird to attend it alone..." I asked while wiping down the kitchen slabs. A strong aroma of Pongal and sambar made him hungry as he walked along the kitchen isle to check if the food was ready.

"No sweetheart! You know I'd get bored there!" he said, straight-faced, browsing through his phone. "Is the breakfast ready? My stomach is growling!" He said rubbing his palm on his stomach.

"Sure!" I said, wiping the extra water and spice powder from the oven. I kind of knew his answer, and hence his reaction didn't surprise me at all.

My phone rang while serving food to Vinod, and the call was from one of my blogger friends. We became friends recently. He was helping me with the graphics trailer for my novel.

"Hey, Pradip! What's up?" I said while eyeing Vinod to lower the TV volume. He reluctantly reduced the volume a little, and I walked to the balcony to hear him better.

"Hello Niharika! I am doing awesome. Actually, I wanted to talk to you regarding something." He said, his voice came clearer with a mix of some outdoor noise. "Sure, tell me…" I walked along the net that saved the balcony from pigeons. Before, the pigeons used to visit more frequently and dirty the balcony floor and walls. It was getting tougher and tougher to keep the balcony clean.

"Hey, if you don't mind, can I tag along to the Orissa trip? I spoke to the organizer, and he called me back saying that everything else can be accommodated except the room. And hence the request." His voice sounded polite as usual.

"You mean you don't have a room to stay there? Hmm…" I just wanted to discuss that with Vinod before allowing another man staying in the same room with me for two days. "Let me call you back on the same. Will that be ok?" I said.

Few little girls in colorful attire giggled and hopped across the walkway as I waved at them.

After a couple of minutes of discussion with Vinod, we decided to agree to share the room with Pradip. Vinod supported me always when it came about helping my friends.

On the day of the fest, when I reached Bhubaneshwar airport in the morning, Pradip was already there, waiting for me. I met him in person for the first time. He looked smart with blue shades and an army green jacket on top of a white t-shirt. His face was round and had a clumsily shaved French beard. He looked much younger than me, which he was anyways, and that suddenly gave me a feeling of being old.

We shook hands, and after a quick chat, we proceeded to the parking lot where a taxi was waiting for us already. We reached the venue, which was a hotel, and in the basement of the hotel, they had a huge banquet hall where the book launch and the rest of the programs were scheduled to take place.

We checked into our room quickly as the program had already started, and people had already gathered in the hall. After getting rid of our luggage in the room, we proceeded to the hall. I wished to change into a saree, but time was crunch, and I couldn't. The organizers offered us breakfast. So we finished eating a few bites before joining the program. A huge poster of mine was positioned at the corner of the hall, which made me very nervous. As I entered, everybody's attention was on me, which made me further anxious. I tried not to show the nervousness and smiled at the people already sitting there. We met a few fellow poets and writers. Pradip and I sat at a table where two more writers were already seated. We spoke to them, and slowly things started to get comfortable. I started to settle down finally when something shocking almost blew me off. Someone just walked past me toward the door that led to the other exit. His face carried a strange smile. I was shocked by seeing him there. My jaw dropped as he smiled at me, and I felt like as if all my nervousness was back again. It was Shamik.

Fuck! What the hell is he doing here?

My mind echoed. I felt as if someone threw a huge load on my chest. My heart thumped. As he walked down the hallway and to the door, I followed him, and we both came out of the venue.

"Hey, what are you doing here?" I shook his hand, and he just coolly flaunted a charming smile at me.

"Why, I think it's open for all... isn't it?" he said, and my anger shot to the peak. I was struggling within my mind to find the reason behind his visit to the fest.

Did he follow me to a fest? Did he lose his mind? Is he obsessed with me? Or is there something else that I am unable to comprehend? Why is he here?

"I know, you must be thinking why I am here?" he said, and I narrowed my eyes, worried and agitated by his sudden visit to the fest.

"Yes...why?" My eyes darted his. A fellow poet waved from the other end, and I had to flaunt a fake smile.

"You know the reason… ask yourself!" his eyes darkened. My shoulder slumped against the wall, my eyes trying to read him.

"Hey, come on you guys! Get in… get in!" The organizer Bishuda's voice came prominent from the porch, and we walked back into the hall.

I was shocked by his surprise visit and struggled to internalize it. I decided to ignore him for the rest of the day. I moved two tables away and eyed Pradip to join me at that table. Shamik remained alone at one table, but soon he made new friends there. His charm never failed to attract people around him. He was extremely sociable, and hence making friends for surviving came very naturally to him. Internally, I was feeling temporarily happy even though I was angry with him for the no-intimation visit to the fest. I was happy because he looked comfortable with his new friends. His talent for socializing with anyone came in handy. He could almost make anyone fall for him. We kept exchanging glances occasionally in between the programs, and my irritation was clear to him. I wanted to tone my agitation down, but somehow it didn't happen, probably due to the overwhelming tight schedule of book launching. Pradip had already started to sense the strangeness in my behavior.

"Is everything alright?" he asked, looking at Shamik.

I nodded.

In the evening, Shamik messaged me to join him in his room. Pradip had ordered a bottle of wine and a plate of appetizers to munch with it as we planned to spend the evening on karaoke activities. When Shamik asked, I told him I would be visiting him in some time. He showed his willingness to come to my room, but I refused by saying that people would start talking wrongly about us if they saw us sharing a room. I somehow didn't want him to see Pradip's presence in my room. As if something stopped me from telling that.

After we sang two songs, I asked Pradip to continue with solo songs and proceeded to Shamik's room. He didn't want to sing alone, but he agreed to take a break instead and watch television. Shamik's room entrance was ajar, and Bishuda and Shamik were smoking cigarettes while conversing on casual topics. As I entered, Shamik ushered me to sit. A strange agony was there in his eyes.

Bishuda got surprised to know that we knew each other already. He took leave after a couple of minutes, leaving us in an eerie silence in the cozy double bed room.

I sat at the corner of the bed as Shamik started a playlist on his phone. Coincidentally, his favorite songs were my favorites too. He lit a smoke and offered me one. I took one cigarette from the pack and poised it between my fingers, waiting for him to light it. He lit it. I leaned against the headboard, which felt pretty relaxing, and songs took over the void air. I wanted to be angry, but instead, I felt relaxed and he looked tired. He kept his head on my lap. I didn't say anything in objection to that. Both waited for the fag to be over, internalizing the lyrics of the sad song. Once the song was over, I slowly moved his head from my lap and walked to leave. He got down from the other side and walked along the footboard to reach me.

"Nihar!" His voice trembled.

"See Shamik, I gotta go now!" my fingers were on the doorknob. But his fingers overlapped mine, stopping me from opening the door.

"Why do you want to leave so soon? Please be here for some more time. We could talk the whole night!" His eyes pleading.

I still couldn't say that Pradip was waiting for me.

"I am tired… I need to take a nap." I said, freeing my hand from his grip. He suddenly pulled me strongly, taking me into his arms. My breasts hit against his chest. I could feel a frail sound at the back of my throat.

"Sorry…" he said, acknowledging awkwardness. His nose touched my nose, playing with my nose pin. My stomach churned. I could feel the heat building in my body. Our lips did not meet, but we could feel each other's breath sharply on the skin. Even the sound of breathing sounded aloud in the quiet empty room. When his lips reached to touch my lips, I pushed him suddenly and went back to the door. He came closer, and I feared the proximity between us. He moved a little away toward the closet.

"Nihar, I want to confess something to you!" his hands were shoved in his pockets, his eyes had a bit of moisture in them.

I followed him to the closet. I kind of saw it coming and could get a strong vibe of the subject he was going to talk about.

He murmured something as my ears started ringing.

"I have fallen for you!"

I stood frozen in front of him for a couple of minutes, speechless, biting my lips in sheer nervousness. I wanted to leave that place because my mind was not ready to hear something like that. But I wasn't sure about my heart. It felt as if a corner of my heart was expecting him to say that, as if it craved for his touch, as if it wanted him to linger his fingers on my cheek, as if it wanted those lips on my lips. But I felt it would be wise to go back to my room. Hence, I left him alone in the room with his feelings and came out to the corridor and then to my room. Even after feeling a sharp pain in my heart, I didn't want to embrace him. My fear and practicality of life and a conscious mind took over my feelings. After entering my room, Pradip asked if everything was alright. I smiled, and then we resumed singing. I knew that I looked off, but Pradip did not ask me any personal queries. Shamik kept messaging me the whole night, but I ignored replying to them, making him emotionally more exhausted.

A day in Chandrabhaga beach and Sun temple:

Our journey to Konark's famous Sun temple was scheduled at 9 AM the following morning, and hence I woke up earlier than my usual. We got ready and gathered near the luxury bus parked at the entrance of the hotel at around 7 AM. I wore a red kurta and black palazzo pant. A pair of dangling oxidized earrings which had a series of green beads hanged from my ear lobes. I slipped in my blue watch, a few colorful bracelets on my wrist, making my rose tattoo less visible. Pradip gave me enough compliments in the morning, telling me that I was looking gorgeous and if I wasn't married and at least a little younger than what I was, he would have definitely proposed to me. I asked him to stop, telling him that through the compliments, he was actually reminding me of my age. He then apologized to me, but it was more like banter. We laughed out loud while exiting the room and grabbed undivided attention from a few of our fellow attendees.

While boarding the bus, I saw Shamik next to the bus, standing, probably either because he was yet to finish his smoke or because he was waiting for me so that he could join me. But I plainly ignored him. My mind didn't want to complicate my already complicated life, and hence I didn't want to encourage the emotions that he had for me. Hence, I walked into the bus and looked for a two-seater with one already occupied seat. I found Neel, whom I met just the previous day. We shared the same table and also a good friendship vibe. He was quiet in nature, kind of a reserved person, and I was not up for much casual chitchat either. So I had chosen him as my co-passenger in the bus. Pradip was a little shocked initially and stared at me as I avoided sitting with him. But soon I messaged and let him know that since he was a blogger and would be busy covering the whole trip into his camera, I decided to sit with Neel. He totally understood me and started capturing one by one everybody through the lenses of his high-end camera. I made a funny face when his camera focus came on me. Shamik got into the bus after stubbing out his cigarette, and I could instantly catch his pale face when he saw me sitting with Neel. I avoided looking at him, and he avoided seeing me and walked past me to the last seat of the bus. He sat with the organizer Bishuda. Neel and I shared a few chocolate biscuits and orange juice. The bus and day both started with positive energy. Everyone's cheerful chitchat filled the bus. Few people sang in between, few cracked silly jokes, and Pradip kept himself busy shooting the whole thing, occasionally sitting on his seat. Neel and I spoke little, once in a while, but we were very comfortable with each other. I found that he was a music lover too, and when he offered to share his earplug with me, I happily grabbed it. Even though I wanted to see, I still didn't look over my shoulder to get a glance of Shamik. I wondered whether he was bored, or he was looking at me, or he was just cursing himself for coming to the fest. But still, I refrained myself from showing any kind of communication with him.

We reached the beach first. Everybody got off the bus and soaked their feet while walking along the seashore. Few people almost bathed in that water, and few stayed totally away just enjoying the view of the morning sea. There were other visitors too apart from our team. Suddenly, the beach was looking filled with people and colors. It looked very lively and vibrant. People captured themselves in selfies, few flaunted funny postures, and few gave reactionless expressions. I fell somewhere in the middle. I walked with Neel along the shore. We took a couple of photos, few with the groups and few singles too. He spoke about his experiences of his previous visits to the same beach, and I listened to them with patience. We became good friends in the course of the trip. I could see Pradip on and off, here and there taking pictures and videos, but I could not locate Shamik. As if he was lost somewhere in the crowd. My eyes were wanting to see him, but why? I feared my own instinct. Even though I was with Neel, my brain was shuffling through the moments with Shamik. No way could I push those thoughts away. My anger on myself kept growing as I took the bottle of water from Neel and gulped almost half a bottle of water from it.

But is the water going to wash away his thoughts? What the hell am I trying to do?

I cursed myself.

“Hey, all ok?” Neel asked, seeing me lost.

“All good. Umm… just thinking if there was a restroom somewhere nearby!”

“Yes, I guess there’s one over there. Come with me!” He walked a little faster as his finger pointed to a small shop. I followed him. The border of my trousers felt heavy from absorbing water and shore sand. We found a well-maintained toilet and water tap and a place to wash legs and I got relief. Even though they charged ten bucks just for washing legs still it was worth going there. I got rid of the sandy feeling from my legs, and so did Neel, and then we proceeded to the bus. I finally saw Shamik there, talking to Bishuda. I felt strangely relieved. As if my mind was wanting something else and my heart was demanding something else. I avoided looking at him and walked into the bus. Neel followed. Everybody got in once again. We started again to our next destination, Konark’s famous Sun temple.

We got off the bus one more time to explore the Sun temple. It was mid-day and started to get hotter then, and I looked for a shade in my white tote bag. When I finally found a shade, I saw Shamik sitting there. I walked to him and sat next to him under the quietness of the huge tree. The rest of the people were a little away, enjoying the rare and exquisite sculptures of the ancient temple.

"What you doing here?" I asked while sitting.

He just smiled, but no answer came from his side. I smiled back and we remained seated there for the next ten minutes.

After the temple trip once we were back to the hotel, we made our ways to the dining hall. Everybody was starving and looked pale and burned in the sun. Pradip, Neel, and I sat at one table and had a quick lunch when I saw a message on my phone.

"Hey, I am leaving in a couple of minutes." It was from Shamik.

That message came like another shock to me. I restlessly started looking for Shamik. "What's wrong?" asked Pradip.

"Nothing! I'll be back!" I faked a smile and got on my feet instantly. I went to the third floor and knocked on his door multiple times, but none responded. Suddenly I started missing him, suddenly a hollowness took over my heart. I rushed to the front desk to inquire if he had checked out, and I was told that he did check out a couple of minutes ago. I rushed to the entrance porch, but he wasn't there.

Did he already leave the venue?

I felt a heaviness. I rushed to the dining hall again and finally saw him having lunch with Bishuda and a few other people. A relief washed over my mind, and I heaved a sigh.

"I need to talk to you!" I said in Bengali, tapping near his shoulder.

"Give me a minute…" he said, looking over his shoulder.

I waited for him. I wanted to stop him from going, but by that time, he wanted to leave the place. It looked like the frustration crossed the threshold of his tolerance. The way I avoided and ignored him was too hard for him to process, and I could realize that, but it was too late by then, and he made up his mind to leave. He wasn't angry with me, but I was still hurt, and then Shamik left.

Chapter 7

My phone rang in the afternoon when I was busy chopping carrots for poriyal. Maids in Delhi were absent half the month, and it was on such a day. Pepper Rasam was steaming, leaving a strong aroma all over my house and probably my neighbors too. Both my maids were absconded for a couple of days due to heavy downpour.

"Hey… what's up?" I said, turning off the burner.

"Are you home? I would like to drop in to discuss a two-minute short film. Of course, if you have time for a brainstorm!" Abhik said as I looked at the wall clock. The time was 2 PM, and I was yet to take my shower.

"Sure! Maybe in an hour? Will that work?"

"Sure! And Thanks!" He hung up without bothering to hear more.

I wrapped up my kitchen work and tidied up the house and had a quick shower before he could stop by. I was just done with my usual praying, lighting a few incense sticks when I heard a strong knock on the door.

"Hey Abhik, please come in!" I ushered him in, and he walked in and sat on the couch, making himself comfortable.

"You have a really nice house! It's spacious, especially for a shoot!" He said, and I smiled acknowledging. I sat next to him.

"So what's the film about?" I asked, putting away the papers from the coffee table.

"Umm... it would be an abstract one where I would like to show how mechanical our lives have become these days... how people are going away from their feelings... both physical and mental, compromising their emotional sides." He said smiling, rubbing his fingers on the rough fabric of our sofa.

"Interesting! Coffee?" I asked without wanting to know the answer and walked to the kitchen to boil milk.

"How's the concept?" He asked sitting there.

"It's great!" I said making my way to the kitchen.

"Sure!" he said. My phone that was laying on the coffee table rang aloud flashing Shamik's face on the screen.

"Hey! You are getting a call..." Abhik looked into the screen, recognizing Shamik's face. I avoided picking up the call. Shamik's face flashed in front of my eyes yet again.

"Hey... are you still in touch with him?" He asked, flaunting a wicked smile. "Interesting... does he call you regularly?"

I just smiled, avoiding to answer his queries. Milk got boiled, and I poured coffee powder into two black ceramic mugs.

He walked to the kitchen, shrugging his shoulders, "what if he wants to sleep with you? Will you?" his face mischievous.

"What?" I laughed out loud. "No!" My hand reached for sugar.

He strolled along the hall and walked to the guestroom, grabbing the coffee mug from the kitchen slab as if it was his own house. I followed. "Can I shoot a film in this house? Your house looks very neat with very little furniture. This would be perfect for my film!" He walked around, and I didn't say no or yes to his question. I came back to the hall, and he followed me. His hand suddenly came from behind my shoulder, embracing my neck in a cozy way. I looked around, "hey!" surprised. He pulled me into an embrace. I was surprised where the coffee was. "What is it?" pushed him little. But he pulled me into his arms again. "Your eyes are intoxicating!" I wanted to pull away again, but he pushed my shoulders quickly pinning my head against the wall. His lips sucked in my lips, and we shared a strong kiss. "No… stop wait!" I turned around facing the kitchen. I told myself to compose. Abhiks hands came from back, hugging me, grabbing my breasts, but I held his hands trying to push them away. But his warm hands came back and made their way through my top, through my bra. I could feel my raised hormones. I could feel his breath on my shoulder, and restless I moaned. "No, I can't!" I murmured. My hands stopped him strongly. He again kissed my lips. I kissed him too. We moved along the walls toward our bedroom. His eyes went to the bedroom door. "Do you have a condom? Let's fuck!" his raw words slivered my soul. His right hand was on my flat stomach pressing me gently against the wall. Suddenly I felt as if I was going to make a mistake, as if I should just stop him from getting further intimate. Shamik's face was constant in front of my eyes.

"Abhik, listen… I think we should stop!" I pulled away and adjusted my messed-up hair and dress. "Let's talk about your film."

"Hmm… but why?" he was disappointed but looked casual about the whole thing.

"I need to think!" I said crisply, and he shrugged. We went back to the sofa and continued talking about his film and other relevant topics. He kept talking about kissing me again, but I avoided giving a response and went back to the discussions.

He left around 5 PM, and I leaned back on the couch thinking about what was happening in my life. Why was I trying to get close to Abhik? Why was I trying to avoid Shamik? Why was I distancing myself from Vinod? All these questions came in rotation when my phone yet again rang with Shamik's call.

I picked up but controlled my mind not to encourage him talking about his emotions toward me. He would have wondered hearing my cold responses but actually I was struggling within my mind to figure things out. I wanted to straighten things out when it was getting more and more coiled up.

The New Year's Eve came with a lot of loneliness and an empty feeling. Vinod was out of town, helping his parents move home when I kept watching Television until late into the night. Abhik messaged me one time inquiring if I wanted to meet him as he was planning to visit an art gallery in South Delhi. I politely declined his proposal, giving an excuse of having a headache. A few of my writer friends had a get-together at a café near our house but somehow I stopped myself from going there too. My house looked empty, filled with an expanse of solitude. I chopped up a few carrots and potatoes and prepared chicken stew for myself and then turned off the stove, bored. I checked myself in the mirror on the way back to the living room. I looked pale, and my skin looked bumpy. I spared a glance at the face scrub but again lost interest. I walked back to the television and looked at my phone. My mind craved to speak with Shamik. But I was hesitant. I didn't want to encourage my inner emotions, the emotions that were going on increasing for him, the feelings that I had no control over. I stared at the phone when Shamik's face surfaced on the screen. It was a call from him. I ignored the first call but the second time, I could not resist myself from picking up.

"Hey! What's up?" I said, sounding unaffected where in actual I was feeling extremely content to hear his voice, as if my soul was just waiting for that one call. "What are you doing? How's your new year eve going?" His voice as soothing as ever.

"Nothing special… Vinod is out of station helping his parents shift their house. It was unplanned and hence he had to leave this morning. I'm just home…" my statement sounded unfinished.

"I am coming! I'm going to catch the flight and will see you in a couple of hours!" his voice sounded demanding, straight, precise.

"What? Why?" I sprang up from the chair. A rush of excitement jolted through my nerves.

"Because I want to see you!" His answer was clear, sharp.

I hung up abruptly.

Walking from one end to another end of the living room, I kept thinking whether I should stop him or let him come. My soul was empty and lifeless as well. I wanted him badly and that was my vital fear. My mind was getting weak for Shamik.

What if I end up kissing him? What if I end up feeling his warmth? What if something more happens? My relentless mind wandered from this to that, and my heart craved to meet him, to talk to him.

He messaged from the airport. I could feel his urge but I couldn't muster up the courage to encourage him for the trip.

"Please don't come!" One final message, and I shut my phone for the night. I knew that my message had broken his heart, but at that time, nothing else came into my mind. Even though all I could think about was Shamik, meeting him and flowing with our emotions felt wrong to me.

The rest of the night was dull, restless, and blank. I didn't get a wink of sleep. Vinod called me when it was midnight, just to wish a short and sweet 'Happy New Year'. Then Niyatidi called, and we spoke for a while. Surprisingly, Shamik's topic came up in that conversation. I had no idea why she was enquiring about him. She asked me if I had met Shamik after moving to India. I denied that fact and told her that I had only spoken with him once over the phone and had never met him in person. My soul felt guilty for everything, including my off behavior toward Shamik.

Three months later:

I visited my mother again when Vinod had to make an official trip to Seattle. Shamik and I started calling each other frequently, and we shared a lot of messages as well. Somehow I wasn't able to take my mind off him. We shared photos and audios. My nights started to get pushed out to late night hours due to chatting with him, sometimes lasting until late into the dawn. One day when I met my best friend Trishna over a casual dinner, I shared my Shamik's story with her. The story made her thoughtful.

"I think he just wants to spend some nights with you!" She drawled, taking a sip from her wine glass.

"I don't think so." I shrugged.

"Come on, Nihar! Is he trying to coax you into an extramarital affair? But why?" She said, staring at the waiter in uniform, standing by the buffet table.

"Stop staring at him!" I said, giving a quick jerk to her wrist.

"Shut up! I'm thinking about your situation!" Trishna frowned.

"What if he really loves me?" I said.

"Oh, come on! We aren't talking about a fairytale and prince charming! It's all lust!" She raised her brows, and I pulled a face.

Lust! Maybe...but! My senses remained occupied thinking about him in a nice way, in a different way, in a loving way.

"Listen!" Trishna shook my elbow. The waiter served us freshly roasted stuffed mushrooms and cold coffee.

"Are you in love with him?" her brows raised.

The waiter's eyeballs toggled between us. I hushed Trishna, and she looked exasperated.

"I don't think so!" my eyes widened. I was trying to refuse it, but deep within, I totally knew that I'd already fallen for him… badly… madly.

"Do you want to get over it…like technically? I have an idea!" Trishna's mischievous smile indicated something naughty.

"How?"

"You just need to sleep with him once! You will get over… trust me," she said coolly.

I almost sprang up from my seat. "What? I can't sleep with him!" Trishna clutched my hand, made me sit again. The waiter thought we were looking for him, and he approached us sharply.

"Anything else, madam?" He said.

"Just the check!" I said. He nodded with a smile.

I sat down.

"Whatever you say, midlife crisis demands physical pleasure only!" She stirred her coffee.

"Stop it, Trishna! I gotta go!" I stood up.

We walked out of the restaurant, and I dropped Trishna at her place on the way to my house. My mind wanted a solution to my radical heart. My brain wanted me to stop thinking about him.

Just the day before going back to Delhi, I told Shamik that I wanted to meet him. I told him that I wanted to spend a day with him. But inside my mind, I had decided that as our last meeting, and we wouldn't see each other ever again. I kept that to myself. I decided to end my journey with Shamik. I was clearly fighting with my destiny.

Flight from my hometown to Delhi:

I was sitting in the eighth row when I saw him walking in. His salt and pepper hair looked stylishly combed, and his tinted glasses perched on the bridge of his nose made him look handsome as usual. He flaunted a usual flirtatious smile at the air hostess, and I almost couldn't control my giggle.

How typical of you!

He saw me from the corner of his narrow eyes while he walked past me, and I blushed like a school kid. Thank God that Rupa, our maid, sitting next to me missed noticing my expressions as Shamik maneuvered to the window seat of the row right behind my row.

I could feel his eyes on me. After a couple of minutes when Rupa fell asleep, I tiptoed to the row and sat next to him. He smiled gorgeously at me, making me blush yet again. He shared his earplugs and wanted me to listen to the song he was listening to. Richard Marx's "Right here waiting..." song was playing. In the course of our off-late intimacy, he had sent me that song multiple times to express his love for me, to express his emotions, and express what he was expecting from me. His fingers brushed my face, making me conscious yet again. I tried to see if Rupa saw the gesture or not.

For the next thirty minutes, I sat next to Shamik, his eyes frequently locking onto my eyes every now and then. His arms touched mine, and so did his soul. He interlaced my fingers with his, increasing my love for him. I wanted to linger in that moment forever. But once Rupa was up, I had to return to my seat. I handed over the earplugs. My fingers lingered on his palm, and my eyes on his eyes. His emotions were obvious, and I was drowning in his eyes.

After the flight arrived in terminal three, our ways parted, but I promised to drop Rupa at my relative's house and meet Shamik in the evening.

I joined him after a quick shower and light makeup. My house was empty, and I decided not to invite him home. So, Shamik remained in the car, waiting for me. I wore a black and white maxi dress and a black woolen shrug. Since it was quite cold in Delhi, I chose to wear my green jacket and black tights underneath my dress; a pair of white shoes and my favorite MK shoulder bag. On the way to the stand-up comedy show, which he had already booked the tickets for, he smiled at me multiple times. I could see the happiness in Shamik's eyes. He kept holding my hand, interlacing my fingers between his like the same way he did in the flight. We entered the venue and got a table for ourselves from where we could enjoy the show and also complete our dinner. The show was great, and so was the food. I could feel that Shamik kept looking at me every now and then. I felt conscious at times, and at times, I felt happy and looked back at him. He smiled, I blushed. We could read each other's minds. He could feel very well that I too started liking spending time with him, I too craved to get close to him, and I too longed for his touch and the look in his eyes. The room was full of the audience. After the show, he took me to a Starbucks located on the ground floor of the same building. Shamik was sure that I would ask him to drop me back home after the coffee, but instead of saying that, and much to his surprise, I asked him to take me out. I shared my wish of spending the night with him. Not in the hotel where he stayed, but just somewhere else where we could sit and talk casually for hours. He agreed, even though he couldn't believe me initially. And hence he asked me twice if I was sure of doing that. I nodded in agreement. His eyes lingered on my face, which started to make me blush.

We hired a taxi and made our way to a place where a whole set of restaurants and bars were open until late at night. The travel took about forty-five minutes, and we reached a fine and urban place. It was a beautiful bar with both indoor and outdoor seating arrangements. The furniture was antique, very apt to my taste. The ambience was loud but perfect. We got a table there, and Shamik ordered our drinks. I was exhausted after a long day and hence decided not to dance. He danced occasionally, and I cheered him up. Everybody present there looked happy and content, lost in their own world. Our evening became night and then late night. At times we sat indoors, and at times outdoors, or at times, we just kept talking and enjoying the music with a smoke in hand, walking casually at the entrance of the bar. I just loved the evening with him. The whole world looked like an illusion to me, and only Shamik felt to be the only truth in the world. When drinking went a bit too much, and I started to wobble, we decided to leave. We again hired a taxi and reached the place where Shamik was staying. I could vaguely see the guard open the main door, and our car drove to the porch. I was much dizzy from the drink. Shamik helped me remove my shoes and jacket. The next couple of minutes were totally blank for me. I had no idea when I dozed off.

Sometime late in the night, when I woke up but still sleepy, I found myself sleeping on his bed. Shamik was next to me, snoring. His face innocent, adorable just like a child. My head felt heavy from a bad headache. I looked around for a water bottle. My frail movement was enough to wake him up.

"Hey! What happened?" He looked at me with his caring eyes.

"Thirsty!" he got up and brought me a glass of water. I saw a glimpse of his bare body and then he pulled on a black t-shirt. My head felt heavy still. I sat up to drink only the water and went back to sleep. I was not completely sleeping when I could feel Shamik walking inside the room. I rolled to the other end of the bed to get the fresh side of the blanket and saw him smoking, looking out the window. He looked attractive. My eyes were fixed on him for some time without his knowledge. I snuggled in the blanket. He asked me if I was hungry; I nodded in denial and kept lying on the bed, my half-opened eyes kept seeing him. He stubbed out the cigarette and slid into the bed from the other side, coming very close to me, almost taking me into his arms. His touch was warm. I loved the way he removed his T-shirt before getting inside the blanket. My heart thumped rapidly when we came closer, when he pulled me closer against his chest. My eyes, little intoxicated, still stared at his eyes trying to freeze his eyes in a frame. We kissed passionately, repeatedly, engrossedly, totally involved in each other. I could feel his warmth going down my veins. His touch was gentle yet strong; there was no haste or desperation in them. I felt as if I could linger in that moment forever. I could feel myself aroused. His eyes constantly looked at my eyes. We cuddled, we moaned... We then hugged and dozed off. When I got up again, Shamik was not there. I blushed to myself. I loved the way I felt. But my head was still aching. He gave me a medicine. We kept looking at each other when he came back to me, and we cuddled again. We talked about many things, happy and content. But I knew that I was going to stop meeting him from the next day.

When I walked to the bathroom and freshened up, he followed me. He rubbed his cheek against my cheek. I loved when he hugged me from back standing in front of the mirror. We got busy again as he fringed through my neck in divine love. My soul just craved for that moment to stay forever, but I stopped him again and moved to the room to get ready.

"Hey, drop me home..." I asked him, and he nodded.

We got ready, occasionally Shamik taking me in his arms. At times, he kissed my forehead. I was falling for him helplessly.

Chapter 8

In the taxi, I remained quieter than usual. Shamik tagged along. Even though it felt absurd, I still decided not to meet him again, not to spend any more nights with him, not to feel the warmth of his touch, knowing that my heart was desperately inclining toward him.

He could figure something was off and tried asking me multiple times. But I refrained myself from telling him that I would not be meeting him after that day. I leaned on his shoulder, exhausted after a fitful sleep and tiring night. I rolled my arms around his arm and settled my head on his chest. Our moments together shuffled through my mind one after another and again, all over again. As if my mind was frozen in a loop where everything was about love, where everything was about Shamik, where everything was about only we two or I would say 'us'.

He asked me if I was doing ok. I nodded. He looked thoughtful too. I knew that the same things were running in his mind too. He asked my food preference, but I said nothing. My hands clutched him tighter at times. My fingers slid through the undone shirt buttons to feel the skin of his chest. He opened one more button to give me more room, and I blushed without his knowledge.

I tried to crack a conversation but kept failing, thinking how he would react when I would say that I wasn't going to meet him anymore. Finally, I mustered up some courage to confess that was there in my mind.

"We will never meet again..." I murmured, and it looked like he figured that out already.

"Why?" His face straight.

"Everything is complicated..." All my statements were unfinished. I could feel a strange push going down my throat. Anxiousness, nervousness, fear of losing Shamik. The whole thing created some kind of war within my core.

He kept quiet, but I could see his anger, his frustration. He was hurt but remained mum.

When I tried to take his hand in mine, lacing my fingers in his, he didn't react. He didn't clutch my palm unlike me. I could feel the heat of his anger.

"I can't!" My eyes went moist. I looked away. I wiped my tears smartly and tried to maintain a normal face. He kept hurting me with his sarcastic words, and I remained quiet, trying not to internalize them, but somehow they kept hurting me, making my chest go heavy.

We stopped at a café to grab a quick lunch. He ordered lasagna, and I ordered a potato salad and my usual coffee. I tried to talk to him, making multiple attempts to convey to him that the feelings that were starting to grow between us should stop immediately. I told him that it may ruin everything in our existing lives, around our lives, and would make things very complicated. His eyes darkened on me at times, shooting me with questions. Few were logical, few sarcastic, and few very raw, just for the purpose of hurting me. My lower gaze refused to reveal my feelings; it refused to show my tears.

"Cheers!" He raised a toast holding his coffee mug. "To our last coffee!" His voice choked. My stomach churned.

After lunch, he dropped me home. Both of us maintained straight faces while parting ways. My head was aching badly, and so as my soul. The car vanished after dropping me, and I walked up the stairs, all eleven floors, instead of the elevator to punish myself for hurting Shamik, for breaking his heart.

Two years later:

I was busy in the kitchen fixing Vinod's lunchbox. The part-time maid had just mopped the kitchen floor, so I was being a little careful not to do any unnecessary walking. My daughters were deep asleep after the second round of Enfamil and diaper change. In baby pink frocks, my twin babies looked like rose petals. Finally, the fourth round of IVF treatment worked. The nanny sat beside the babies keeping an occasional eye on them. Vinod took his own sweet time to get ready when I placed his usual breakfast, bread, omelet, and fruit salad on the coffee table in front of the television.

My phone was left carelessly on the kitchen counter, on top of a book that I had started reading since a couple of days. A flashy notification popped up with no sound. I cocked my head to take a look at the notification.

"Nihar, a glass of water please... urgent!" Vinod called out. I was kind of sure that he had bitten a piece of chili from the omelet.

I rushed with a glass of cold water.

"Honey, please cut them into smaller chunks, please!" he downed a full glass of water, spilling little drops on his just-pressed brown formal shirt.

I pulled a face instantly. "Slow!" I rubbed his back as he took a few pieces of cut fruits and got up from his chair, making his way to the shoe rack.

"Finish it, Vinod!" I almost screamed.

"No time..." He slammed the door on the way out, leaving a huge echo in the corridor. My part-time maid smiled on the way out after finishing her chores.

I got busy cleaning the kitchen when a notification caught my eyes. I grabbed my phone, turned on the fan, and sat beside my daughters but on the floor.

"Hey! Fancy a coffee?" It was a message from Shamik.

A sudden feel of happiness rushed through my mind. I smiled broadly, confusing the nanny who was sitting, bored, next to my asleep twins.

I smiled again from ear to ear.

"Bani, can you stay home for an extra hour in the afternoon and take care of the babies? I just need to meet an old friend of mine." I looked at her seeking confirmation.

"Sure madam! You don't worry." She smiled, confident.

I lied down flat on the floor with the phone on the high of my chest. My face maintained the same smile as I shuffled through the memories yet again.

“Reader’s Café at 2 pm…” my reply to Shamik.

www.ingramcontent.com/pod-product-compliance
Lightning Source LLC
LaVergne TN
LVHW041159150826
845673LV00001B/220

9798892338431